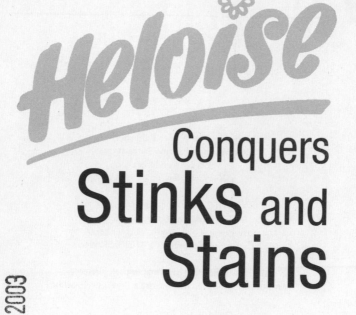

Conquers
Stinks and
Stains

A PERIGEE BOOK

A Perigee Book
Published by The Berkley Publishing Group
A division of Penguin Putnam Inc.
375 Hudson Street
New York, New York 10014

Copyright © 2002 by Heloise, Inc.
Text design by Tiffany Kukec
Cover design by Dorothy Wachtenheim
Cover photo copyright © Michael Keel

First edition: November 2002

Visit our website at www.penguinputnam.com

Library of Congress Cataloging-in-Publication Data

Heloise.
Heloise conquers stinks and stains / Heloise.
p.   cm.
Includes index.
ISBN 0-399-52842-3
1. Spotting (Cleaning).   2. Home economics.   I. Heloise.   II. Title.

TX324 .H45 2002
648—dc 21   2002030341

Printed in the United States of America

10 9 8 7 6 5 4 3 2 1

Note: The information in this book is true and complete to the best of our knowledge. All recommendations on parts and procedures are made without any guarantees on the part of the author or publisher. The author and publisher disclaim any liability incurred in connection with the use of this information.

Dedication

Dedicated to our two sweet dogs Black Jack and Sauvignon who went to Doggie Valhalla in September and December of 2001. You each brought happiness and many smiles into our lives.

Please visit my website, www.Heloise.com, to see photos of our two pals.

Contents

Part 4: Carpets, Rugs, and Floors

Part 5: All Around the House

Contents

Acknowledgments

This book could not have been done without the always upbeat and extremely capable Merry Clark, Editorial Director of Heloise Inc. Thanks ever so much for being such a trouper as well as a superb editor, I treasure our friendship. My office group, Joyce, Jane, Kelly, Ruth and Brucette, who as always stayed to the bitter end getting our book done! John Duff of Penguin Putnam who gave us the title *Stinks and Stains*. I had always called it *Odors and Stains*, but I love this one! You are just the best to work for.

And, never last or least my darling (and cute) husband, David, who puts up with all the work that goes into a book, not to mention book tour. You are the best thing in my life—hope I am in yours.

Heloise
Hintologist

Introduction

Stinks and stains, odors and spots, smells and ugly blots! No matter what you call them, they are a part of our lives, and have been from the beginning of time. I bet the cave guys and gals really had major problems with stinks and stains!

When I started working with my mother, the original Heloise, who started her newspaper column in February of 1959, the questions were pretty much the same as they are today: How do I get ballpoint ink out of a shirt? My garbage disposal smells, what do I do? I spilled wine on the tablecloth, help! My pet had an "accident" on the carpet, what can I use to get the stain out? Even though we have new cleaning products and materials, many of the answers are the same today as they were more than 40 years ago. Use soap and water, blot don't rub, rinse well, and keep working at that stain. Some stain removal just takes time!

I grew up in a "Heloise" household, where my mother had

her office at home; I learned that the simple basics are the guiding principle in stain removal, and odor busting. Hint: *Always* test the stain removal agent first on a small area and *don't* use the strongest or harshest cleaning solution first. Start with the mildest, then work toward the stronger solution. When all else fails, cover it up! Use an appliqué, sew on a patch, put a pin over it, throw on a scarf, or move the furniture and get a throw rug! I am Heloise and I still have a carpet stain I can't get out! It happens to the best of us, so don't sweat it if you can't fix it.

Thanks to all of you who have followed *Hints from Heloise* over the years. I plan on being here for you in the decades to come. I look forward to tackling new stinks and stains in the future—you can bet they will be there.

Hugs,
Heloise

Stinks & Stains Etiquette

WHAT SHOULD YOU DO?
CHOOSE ANY OF THE "OPTIONS" LISTED BELOW:

1. If you create bad odors?

   ☐ Walk away quickly or look at your husband or wife and say loudly, "Honey!"
   ☐ Scold your children or pets!
   ☐ Admit to being the guilty party and try to correct the situation with perfume or room deodorizer.

2. If you notice a bad smell in someone else's house?

   ☐ Let everyone know in a loud voice that there is a terrible smell.
   ☐ Embarrass your host with your big mouth.

☐ Depending on how close you are to the hostess, let her know privately that there is a smelly problem.

3. If you discover a noticeable rotten odor while you have guests in your home?

☐ Pretend it doesn't exist.
☐ Blame the dog, the children, your husband or wife.
☐ Try to locate it ASAP and handle the problem.

4. If a guest in your home makes a bad smell or smells bad?

☐ Tell your guest he needs to go to the bathroom and put on more deodorant.
☐ Depending on how well you know your guest, delicately let the person know as they may not be aware that there is a problem.

5. If you smell horrible odors in the office?

☐ Blame your office mate, the boss or the company management.
☐ Report it to building management, the office manager or your boss.

6. Spill something when visiting someone else's house?

☐ Ignore the mess you've created and go on as if nothing has happened.
☐ Fess up immediately and offer to help clean it up.

Stinks & Stains Etiquette

7. If you knock over a glass or get food on your clothes in a restaurant?

☐ Make a big deal out of it and call the waiter over to complain and threaten not to leave a tip.

☐ Quietly dab the stain with plain water, using your napkin to remove as much of the food as you can as quickly as you can.

8. If you see your children making a stain mess at a friend's house?

☐ Blame your hosts' children for it and don't scold your own.

☐ Let your hosts know immediately and get your child to offer to help clean it up.

9. If you spill liquids on your computer or the carpet at the office?

☐ Do nothing, hoping your computer won't work and you can get a break!

☐ Get help right away and try to correct the situation.

Stinks & Stains Etiquette

PART ONE

Stinks

Holding Your Nose Is Not the Only Option

Life is full of aromas and scents; some lovely, others not. If you have a house filled with children, pets and lots of activity, awful odors will abound. Let's face it: many of them stink! They always seem to happen when you least expect it or when you expect company! Talk about adding stress to already busy days.

So often those ugly smells are such a shock! Where did they come from? As experience has taught you, it's always best to deal with them right away. If you don't, they only get worse.

Keep Heloise's cheap, home-style odor busters on hand all in one place and ready-to-use in urgent smelly crises. I like products that are environmentally safe, such as baking soda, vinegar and lemon juice. They do a great job in masking and removing household smells. But there are many other odor solutions in your kitchen cabinets that many readers have shared with me. And now I'm happy to share them with everyone in this book.

My mother, the original Heloise, passed on many words of wisdom to homemakers—and to me. In one of my favorite quotes from her, she said, "Budget your energy doing only what you can. Life is priceless, so learn to enjoy it. Learn to do things the easy way. Take every shortcut you can find." It is my hope that the collective wisdom gathered here will give you the shortcuts and easy solutions for tasks around that house that just *have* to be done. So let's deal with those smelly problems pronto!

Stinks A-to-Z

AIR FRESHENER: Conserve the power of small plastic air fresheners by pulling back the foil only halfway. The aroma will last longer and won't overpower a small room.

AIR FRESHENER (homemade): Soak a cotton ball with peppermint, vanilla, orange, lemon extract or oil of cloves. Place it in a small, clean, glass jar, the lid of which has been punched with holes. Secure tightly. Place in the smelly room out of the reach of small children and pets. CAUTION: Extracts are strong concentrates with high alcohol content. Do not let the extract touch granite, marble, painted surfaces or wood.

AIR FRESHENER IN A VACUUM: Grab a handful of your favorite spiced tea (loose or in a tea bag) and toss into the vacuum bag. While you clean, it will give the house a nice spicy smell.

AQUARIUM SMELLS: Too much algae growth and uneaten fish food can give the tank an odor. Clean out leftover fish food with a turkey baster, *used only for this purpose*. Monitor the aquarium and clean it on a regular basis to prevent smells.

ASHTRAY: To deodorize ashtrays, fill them partially with a small amount of clay-type cat-box litter or baking soda. It will help to reduce odor and to extinguish the cigarettes completely.

> ### Reader Letter of Laughter
>
> *When I was a child, I was helping my dad wax his car. He said I should use a little more elbow grease, so I started rubbing my elbow on the car. He laughed and teased me about it for a long time.*

BABY BOTTLE: Get rid of that awful sour-milk smell by filling bottles with warm water and a teaspoon of baking soda. Let sit overnight. Then wash and sterilize as usual. Note: To prevent this from happening, immediately after baby has finished, rinse the bottle with cold water and put a teaspoon of baking soda into it and fill with cold water. Let soak until you need the bottle again.

BASEMENT MILDEW: Basements always seem to have high moisture or dampness, which causes mildew to thrive and grow. Your first line of defense is to keep the basement as dry as possible and have good air circulation.

Place activated charcoal, which you can find at a pet supply, aquarium or large home-improvement store in open containers in the areas that need it the most, or put the charcoal into old panty hose and hang in a corner, where you can't hit your head! You also can use baking soda or commercial products.

Stinks

BATHROOM SINK: Pour vinegar down the drain, because it kills bacteria that may be growing in the trap. Or, pour a cup of household bleach down the drain, wait for an hour; then flush with lots of cold water. If this doesn't work, call a plumber because it could be a serious problem.

BATHROOM SURFACES: To deodorize bathroom surfaces, wipe with a mixture of ½ cup borax to 1 gallon of water.

BEDSHEETS: When you take sheets from the storage cabinet and discover they are musty, toss them into the dryer with a fabric-softener sheet for up to ten minutes. Keep linens smelling fresh by placing a fabric-softener sheet or bar of white soap in the linen closet. Don't let the fabric-softener sheet touch fabric because it may leave an oily spot.

BIRDCAGE: To keep odors from building up, place several layers of newspaper or grocery store paper bags on the bottom of the cage. Remove and replace with new sheets every other day.

BLEACH (on hands): Of course, you should wear rubber gloves to prevent this. But to remove the odor of bleach, wash your hands with soap and water, rinse and then dab with a little apple cider vinegar, toothpaste or mouthwash.

BOOKS (musty): If you see mildew, first vacuum the books using the brush attachment. Gently vacuum the pages. If they are musty, sprinkle each page with baking soda or a bit of cornstarch. Place in a plastic bag for a week or so to absorb the odors. Remove the books outdoors and turn them upside down and shake out the cornstarch or baking soda. Always store books in a dry spot. To prevent a musty smell, put plain charcoal into an old sock with the books. Do not store books in a damp basement.

BOTTLE/JAR DEODORIZING: If they have a bad smell after washing, soak them overnight in a mixture of half vinegar and half water. Rinse well. Be sure to wash the lid in hot soapy water and store with the lid off.

BREATH DEODORANT: For a surefire homemade remedy for bad breath, gargle with a solution of 1 teaspoon baking soda to ½ glass of warm water. At a restaurant, eat the parsley. Chew, chew, chew then wash it down with a big gulp of water—swishing around a bit to get the parsley flakes off your teeth! Parsley is a natural breath cleanser, and nutritious, too.

BURNED FOOD: Put several slices of lemon or ¼ cup vinegar in a saucepan half-filled with water, bring to a boil and let cook for a few minutes. (Watch carefully so it doesn't boil dry and create yet another disgusting smell and ruin your pot.)

BUTCHER BLOCK DEODORIZER: Sprinkle baking soda on the top of the block and scrub with a clean, damp sponge. Rinse well. Or, you can sprinkle it with salt and scrub with a lemon, and then rinse well. To renew the surface, apply a light coating of *mineral oil* (NOT vegetable oil) and wipe up with a paper towel.

CABBAGE: To kill cabbage-cooking stink try one of these methods:

- Drop a whole walnut into the boiling water, shell and all

- Put a heel of bread on top

- Add a splash of vinegar to the cooking water

- Place a bowl of vinegar next to the stove to absorb the odor.

CAN OPENER: Wash a nonelectric can opener in warm, soapy water after every use to get rid of food bits that harbor bacteria and smell bad. Clean the blades or cutters of an electric can opener with an old toothbrush dipped in baking soda.

CAR/AUTOMOTIVE VEHICLES (musty): In damp climates, cars can get that musty smell. To eliminate it:

1. Clean upholstery on a regular schedule with dry commercial upholstery cleaners, which can be found at grocery, hardware, auto or home-improvement stores.

2. Remove plastic floor mats and scrub with a mixture of half vinegar and half water. Be sure to rinse well and let dry completely in the sun before putting back into the vehicle.

3. Use a spray-type carpet cleaner to shampoo or clean the carpeting, but do not let the backing get wet.

4. Spray the trunk and ceiling inside the vehicle with a commercial deodorizer.

CAR DEODORIZER: Pour baking soda into the ashtray and keep another box, punched with holes, under the front seat. Not only will it help deodorize, but it will also come in handy if there's a fire because it extinguishes small flames.

CARPET: For a quick fix of general carpet odor, sprinkle baking soda over it. Leave on for at least 30 minutes; then vacuum.

CARPET (musty): This may be a sign that the carpet or rug is damp. Be sure to check the underpadding to see if it is damp. Take the rug and padding outside to dry in the sun if you can. If you cannot remove the rug, try to dry it with a fan. If the damp area is small, use a hair dryer set on cool. Turn on ceiling fans, or use box fans. Also, if you have air-conditioning, turn it on to the lowest temperature.

CARPET DEODORIZER: Sprinkle baking soda, with a flour sifter or your hands, over the carpet that needs freshening. Allow it to sit for at least 20 minutes, then vacuum. If you notice lightly soiled spots, rub a small amount of cornstarch into them, before you vacuum. Note: To extend a commercial carpet deodorizer, mix equal amounts of baking soda and the commercial product to double the volume.

CAR TRUNK DEODORIZER: If the trunk is covered with carpeting, sprinkle lots of baking soda over it, leave on for several days and then vacuum.

CAT BEDDING: To deodorize, toss a handful of baking soda onto the bedding in between washings and then vacuum. Don't do this if your cat is on a salt-restricted diet because baking soda is SODIUM BICARBONATE.

CAT LITTER BOX (cleaning): To eliminate odor, empty all the litter out of the box. Pour about ½ inch of vinegar into the box, add a healthy dose of baking soda and top off with several inches of water. Stir to mix well. Let sit for several hours then empty and wash with hot, soapy water. Allow to dry outside if the weather permits. Keep an air freshener in the room where the litter box is.

CAT LITTER BOX (deodorizing): To deodorize, before putting cat litter into the box, pour a layer of baking soda on the bottom. This will help to subdue odors until you change the litter. Note: Cats are picky and some may not like baking soda. If they are not using the box, don't use baking soda.

CAT SPRAYS: To remove the smell if a cat sprays inside, use an enzyme-based commercial product made for this purpose. It is available at your vet or pet store. If odor remains, mask it with potpourri or a room deodorant spray.

CAT URINE ON CARPET: To remove the smell, use an old, thick towel (one designated for this kind of use) to blot up all of the urine ASAP. Then rinse the area with cool water, and apply a warm detergent solution. Follow with a solution of ⅓ vinegar and ⅔ cool water. Blot between each step with a paper towel. Rinse and blot dry. You can also use a commercial enzyme-based pet stain cleaner. Or, depending on the fabric, treat persistent stains with 3 to 5 percent hydrogen peroxide. Test a small hidden area first. Be careful of bleaching and rinse quickly.

CAUTION: Although professionals recommend using a diluted ammonia solution as a final step, I don't because it smells like urine and may encourage your pet to commit repeat offenses!

CEDAR CHEST: See MOTHBALL

CIGARETTE: (See also SMOKE.)

- In draperies: Have them professionally cleaned or spray them with a fabric freshener. Depending on the draperies, they can also be placed in the dryer on the "fluff" cycle with a fabric softener sheet to freshen them.

- In soft furnishings: Have professionally cleaned or spray them with a fabric freshener.

- In mattresses: Use an aerosol fabric or upholstery odor-removal spray on the mattress first. Then put the mattress and the box spring outside in the fresh air and sunshine, if possible. If it still reeks, you may have to clean it again with a cleaning machine, which can be rented from your local rent-all. *Follow instructions precisely.* If the odor is inside the mattress, you may need to rent or buy an air purifier machine that produces ozone, which is what many fire restoration companies use. Close the room and turn on the machine and hope for the best!

- In cars: Empty ashtrays often and then pour several tablespoons of baking soda into them. Then sprinkle baking soda on the upholstery and carpet and vacuum thoroughly. Leave the windows open when possible.

- In wooden cabinets: Clean cabinet first. Put small dishes of either vinegar *or* baking soda (not combined) on shelves to help absorb odor. This may take several days or weeks. If there's still odor, put a bag of cedar shavings inside to give it a pleasant aroma.

CLOSET (mildew or musty): Place a clean coffee can or other container filled with activated charcoal in the back of the closet. Or: Use a closet dehumidifier, which is available at hardware or drugstores.

CLOSET DEODORIZER: To keep a closet sweet-smelling, mix 3 to 4 teaspoons of your favorite spice with a box of baking soda. (I like cinnamon and nutmeg!) Pour the mixture into several clean plastic margarine tubs, punch holes into the lids and put in the back of the closet or on the shelves.

Or, give a walk-in closet a good aroma by walking into it immediately after you sprayed yourself with cologne; the scent will linger. But, do NOT let any of the spray get onto hanging clothing because it might stain or damage delicate fabrics.

Leave doors open when possible.

CLOSET FRESHENER: Pour several tablespoons of fresh, unused ground coffee into a couple of old clean socks and hang them in the closet to help prevent that musty odor. (See also AIR FRESHENER [homemade].)

CLOTHES: If your washables smell, add ½ cup household non-sudsing ammonia or baking soda to the rinse cycle.

CLOTHES (storing): To prevent musty smells when you put your clothes away for the season, place used fabric-softener sheets or wrapped bars of soap into the drawers.

CAUTION: Do not let the fabric-softener sheets come in direct contact with silk or other materials, because they could stain.

CLOTHES HAMPER: To prevent odors, fill a clean paper coffee filter with baking soda and securely tape shut and put into the bottom of the hamper. Replace it every couple of weeks. Or, sprinkle baking soda directly into the hamper. Place fabric-softener sheets or perfume sampler strips in the bottom of the hamper.

COFFEE CUP/MUG/TUMBLER: To prevent odors, rinse out your cup ASAP after use. To remove the coffee smell, pour 1 teaspoon of baking soda into the cup and fill with warm water. Let it stand at least ½ hour or so and then scrub with a brush or sponge. You may have to repeat this process.

COOKING: To eliminate general cooking odors, boil a mixture of 1 cup water and 1 to 2 tablespoons vinegar in a saucepan on the stove. CAUTION: Watch carefully so the pan does not boil dry.

Stinks

To give the whole house a good smell, add cinnamon (a whole stick or sprinkle of powdered) to the water/vinegar solution.

COOKING (corned beef): To eliminate that smell, add a tablespoon or so of vinegar to the water while boiling.

COOLER: Before you store a cooler, sprinkle a generous amount of baking soda into it and stuff with crumpled newspapers to prevent a musty smell. Also, try to store with the lid propped open to allow the air to circulate. When you are ready to use it again, dump the soda into the kitchen sink. Run lots of water and the drain will be refreshed too!

CUTTING BOARDS: To remove smells like onion or garlic from a wooden cutting board, sprinkle with salt and then rub the surface with a cut lemon or lime. Then wash with warm soapy water, rinse and re-season with mineral oil if the board is wood.

DEODORANT: For a natural deodorant, try one of these:

- Apply baking soda to underarms with a dusting puff. (This hint came from my mother, and is still good today.) You can keep it in a decorative box in your bathroom.

- Dab underarm area with apple cider or white vinegar. It kills bacteria and has no smell when it dries.

DIAPER PAIL: Sprinkle baking soda in the bottom of the pail before you put diapers in and also after! Dispose of dirty diapers ASAP and AOAP (as often as possible).

DISHWASHER: First you have to find out where the odor is coming from. Look inside the dishwasher to examine the drain hose and the bottom reservoir for food particles or residues that may be trapped there. Gunk and grease can accumulate. If the water isn't hot enough to wash it away, this stuff can cause the odor. Using a large wad of paper towels, clean out the reservoir. Be careful, because there could be broken glass or other sharp bits.

The odor may be coming from clogged kitchen drainpipes or sewer lines. If you suspect this, call a plumber.

To prevent odors, clean the dishwasher every month or so by pouring either ½ cup bleach or 1 cup household vinegar into the detergent cup and run through a cycle. There are also commercial dishwasher freshener products that can do the job, too. In between use, pour baking soda on the bottom of the dishwasher to help control the odor.

DOG BED DEODORIZING: Sprinkle a little baking soda over the bed to neutralize odor until washing, which you should do often to keep doggie smells to a minimum. Don't use if your dog is on a salt-restricted diet because baking soda is SODIUM BICARBONATE.

DOGGIE DEODORANT I: Dogs can get that stinky doggie smell in between baths. To help eliminate it, rub baking soda into the fur (don't get into eyes); leave on for about 10 minutes and brush out. Your precious pup will be welcome inside again! But don't apply to your pet if it's on a salt-restricted diet as baking soda is SODIUM BICARBONATE.

Stinks

DOGGIE DEODORANT II: Make a doggie spritzer by mixing 32 ounces of water with 2 capfuls of a fragrant bath oil and pour into a spray bottle. Spritz your pet's coat and rub in. CAUTIONS: Be sure to label the bottle of this homemade mixture. Don't spray into dog's eyes or ears!

DOWN/FEATHER-FILLED COMFORTERS: These household items often get a musty odor so just toss them into the dryer (on the air cycle only) with a fabric-softener sheet (if you want to add fragrance) for several minutes with a tennis ball or two! If this doesn't do the job, take them to a professional cleaner that has the special equipment to clean this kind of bedding.

DRAINS: Try this homemade mixture to keep drains fresh smelling. (But note that it does NOT unclog drains): Pour ½ cup baking soda into the drain and then pour 1 to 2 cups of vinegar down the drain. Let sit and bubble for several minutes; turn on the hot water and let it run for a minute or so and finally flush out the drain with lots of cold water. To kill germs that could be causing the smell, pour ½ cup liquid household bleach or 1 cup vinegar down the drain. Let sit for about 20 minutes, then flush with water.

FART: Wave your hand to disperse bad odor or use a room deodorant spray. In the bathroom, light a match, then blow it out to get rid of bodily function smells.

FEATHER PILLOWS: Open just one corner of the ticking to empty feathers into a large, deep box and set outside in the sun. Fluff feathers occasionally. Wash pillowcase before refilling with feathers.

FIREPLACE: Odors from the fireplace may be caused by the kind of wood burned or a buildup of creosote, soot, moisture, or even a poor animal caught in the flue. First scrub the fireplace walls and ceiling with a solution of vinegar or a mild bleach and water. Then sprinkle clay-type cat litter and let sit for several days to absorb odor. If odors aren't gone, call a professional chimney sweep.

If the smoky odors from the fireplace have permeated the room, do one or all of the following:

- Allow the ash to cool completely and remove. (Ash is good for the garden!)

- Dry-clean or wash draperies and curtains.

- Shampoo carpeting.

- Change filters in the furnace or air conditioners.

- Spray furniture with a fabric deodorant.

FISH: To eliminate the cooking odor of fish in the kitchen, simmer a solution of ½ cup vinegar and ½ cup water in a saucepan on low heat. Or: Put a cup of vinegar in an open container on the kitchen counter.

FISH SMELL ON HANDS: At home: Squeeze lemon or lime juice over hands and wash well, or pour apple cider vinegar over hands and rub in. A dab of toothpaste or a bit of mouthwash rubbed into your hands will also do the job.

Before you go on a fishing or camping trip: Soak small towels in a mixture of lemon juice and water, then put into resealable

Stinks

plastic bags and store in the freezer. Pop them into the cooler when you head out. By the time you've caught your limit, the towels will be thawed and ready to use.

FLOOR SAFE: If you have room inside the safe, place a small box of baking soda at the back of the safe to prevent musty odors. If this isn't working, try a desiccant or silica gel, which can be found at craft stores. Open the door and air it out occasionally.

FOOT ODOR: Take these steps to prevent smelly feet:

- Wash feet completely with soap and hot water daily and dry well. Apply an antiperspirant foot spray or powder or baking soda to your feet. For your children, make a dusting box by taking a shoe box and filling with ½-inch layer of baking soda. Let kids step in it, shake their feet (over the box!) to get rid of the loose baking soda and then put on their socks.

- Wear shoes made of leather or canvas, which absorb perspiration and allow feet to "breathe." During hot months wear sandals.

- Spritz hot, tired and sweaty feet with a bit of cologne or wipe feet with a packaged moist towelette—and you don't even have to remove panty hose to do this!

FREEZER DEODORIZER: Use a solution of 4 tablespoons baking soda in 1 quart of water to wipe the wall and bottom of the freezer then rinse and wipe dry. If you notice a stain that has not been removed, DO NOT use an abrasive cleaner because it can damage the surface. Instead, pour baking soda onto a wet sponge and scrub the area. Place an open tub or box of baking soda in the freezer compartment for continuous deodorizing.

FREEZER FOOD SPOILAGE: To remove the stench from spoiled food as a result of an electricity failure, first, dispose of the spoiled food. Clean the freezer with soap and water. Then rinse with a solution of about 1 cup vinegar to 1 gallon water. Pour clay-type cat litter in open containers or pour lemon extract on cotton balls and place inside the freezer. Leave closed for several days.

GARBAGE CANS: To prevent odors, place a fabric-softener sheet or perfume sample strip into the bottom of the can before you put the plastic garbage bag inside.

GARBAGE DISPOSAL: Drop in a handful of sliced citrus peels (lemon, lime, orange or grapefruit), with lots of running water and grind; flush with water. Or, add several drops of peppermint or other extracts along with water to deodorize it.

Versatile Vinegar

Did you know that vinegar has been around for more than 10,000 years? It has been used as a preservative, a condiment, a beverage, and during World War I to treat wounds. It's legend that Cleopatra made a wager that she could consume a fortune in a single meal! How? It's said she dissolved a precious pearl in the vinegar and drank it! Who knows for sure?

GARLIC ODORS IN PLASTIC STORAGE CONTAINERS: If they've taken on a garlicky odor, wash in hot, soapy water and then give them a vinegar rinse and dry. Stuff a crumpled sheet of newspaper inside and put the lid on securely. Leave for a day or two.

Stinks

GLASS JARS: Wash well in hot, soapy water and rinse completely. Fill with a solution of half vinegar and half water. Let sit overnight with the lid off. Rinse and dry. You also can fill jar with crumpled newspaper and let stand overnight to get rid of smells. Clean the lid with hot soapy water.

GYM BAG: Before you put your exercise clothes into the bag, sprinkle baking soda over the bottom to help absorb the odors of the clothing after you've exercised. Also, keep perfume strips or samples in the bag to mask stinks.

GYM CLOTHES: Wash as soon after you exercise as you can. Pre-soak garments in a solution of water and non-chlorine bleach with enzymes. (CAUTION: Test first for colorfastness and read directions for right proportions.) During the wash or rinse cycle, add ½ cup baking soda, which acts as a natural deodorizer.

HANDS: To remove smells on hands, scrub with toothpaste or rinse hands with mouthwash. To avoid smelly hands, wear rubber or thin plastic gloves when working with onions, garlic or other strong smelling items.

ICE CUBES: Automatic maker: First, check the ice-cube bin because the cubes could be picking up odors from the refrigerator. Use activated charcoal (found at pet stores) as a deodorizer for the refrigerator. Put several pieces into cleaned-out, plastic butter tub, replace lid and punch holes in it and place inside the refrigerator. Wash bin with cool soapy water. Rinse and dry well.

KITCHEN SINK: Getting rid of odors can be an ordeal. Try these ideas:

- The sink area may still smell because there's a buildup of bacteria in the drain. Pour a cup or so of bleach into the sink and allow it to sit for 20 minutes to kill bacteria that may be growing inside. Run cold water for at least a minute to clear the drain.

- If you have a garbage disposal, the rubber splashguard may be slimy and need to be cleaned. Run water. Add several drops of liquid dishwashing detergent and use a round brush or a toilet brush (just for this purpose) to scrub the guard well; go up and down and all around to get it clean. Then run more water.

- Examine sink stoppers and splashguards; they can get grungy and harbor bad odors. Because they are inexpensive, you can replace often.

LAUNDRY: If dirty clothes have a really strong odor, add ½ cup baking soda to the rinse cycle and make certain that you don't overload the washer because clothes won't be able to move around enough for cleaning. Also, try a second rinse cycle.

> ### Letter of Laughter
>
> *"I noticed my 12-year-old daughter was ironing her shirt one morning before school. As I took a closer look, I realized that she did not even have the iron plugged in. I asked her why she didn't have it on and her reply was, 'The tag says to use a cool iron.'"*

LAUNDRY FRESHENER: To get fresher laundry, add 1 cup of white vinegar to the final rinse water. Some say it will make laundry softer and fluffier.

LINEN STORAGE: To prevent stale odors and to give sheets and towels in your storage closet a fresh scent, place wrapped bars of soap between the sheets and towels.

LUGGAGE: If your suitcase has been stored away and has a musty odor, try these odor solutions:

Stinks

- Open up and put outside in the sun. Mother Nature just may do the trick.

- Put a shallow box filled with cat-box deodorizer into the suitcase and shut the lid. Let it sit for a day or two.

- Place a fabric-softener sheet or several wrapped bars of fragrant soap inside, close and let sit for a couple of days.

- Stuff with crumpled newspaper to absorb odor. Replace with fresh newspaper every other day until smell is gone.

- Fill a small container, such as a cleaned-out plastic margarine tub, with activated charcoal (found in pet stores). Poke holes in lid and cover. Leave in suitcase and close.

CAUTION: Do not store luggage in the basement, where there may be dampness.

LUNCH BOX: Moisten a piece of stale bread or paper towel with vinegar and place in the lunch box overnight. In the morning, wash well and dry. Leave top open to air out.

MATTRESS: To remove "accident" odor, first absorb as much of the urine as you can with paper towels. Sponge—not soak—the stained area with a solution of half vinegar and half water. Dry the area with a hair dryer on low or cool. When dried, spray with an aerosol fabric freshener. If you can get the mattress outside to a sunny spot, let it air out. (See also CIGARETTE.)

MICROWAVE: To clean and eliminate odor, combine 2 tablespoons baking soda with 1 cup of water in a large microwave-safe bowl. Place in the microwave and turn it on high for 2 to 3 minutes. This will soften the spills so you can wipe them up and the smells will be gone! Be careful when you open the door because the steam will be hot.

MICROWAVE (burnt popcorn): Burnt popcorn odor is such a disgusting and lingering smell! Try this: In a large microwave-safe bowl, combine 1½ cups of water, ½ chopped lemon and 4 to 5 cloves. Bring mixture to a boil. Let it sit in the microwave for 10 to 15 minutes before you remove the bowl. Leave the door of the microwave open to further air it out.

Microwave Magic

To get a pleasant aroma throughout the house, combine 1 cup of water and 2 teaspoons of pumpkin-pie spice—or any combination of spices to your taste—in a large microwave-safe bowl and cook on high until it boils. When it reaches the boiling point, cook for a minute or two. Or, combine 6 whole cloves and a half lemon in a cup of water and microwave on high for 2 to 3 minutes. CAUTION! Always allow the liquid to cool before removing the bowl.

MILK SPILLS: In the car, whether it's inside or in the trunk, spilled milk leaves an unforgettable odor—especially if the car has been sitting out in the hot sun! Use an all-purpose carpet cleaner, or wipe—not soak—with a solution of vinegar and water. Let dry and sprinkle everything with baking soda. If it still smells, treat with special fabric spray. Or: Place activated charcoal, or freshly ground coffee in a container with holes punched into the lid and put under the seats or in the trunk. No Luck? You may have to replace the carpet.

MOP (floor): Soak the mop for several hours in a mixture of 1 quart water and 4 tablespoons baking soda. Rinse well, squeeze out and hang to dry.

Stinks

MOTHBALLS: This is a tough one to get rid of. Give these hints time to work—and you may have to repeat:

- Clothing: Hang colorfast garments outdoors in the bright sun, and others in the shade. Or: Put clothing into the dryer on fluff dry and toss in several fabric softener sheets. Do NOT use heat, which can set the vapors. Washables can be done with a powdered laundry detergent and rinsed with fabric softener.

- Wooden furniture: If the weather permits, leave the chest or drawer outdoors in the sun for several days as the odor dissipates. Or: Try a wood cleaner (available at home-improvement or hardware stores) to clean the inside of the drawers. Let dry completely before replacing clothing.

  If your cedar chest smells of mothballs, move it to a well-ventilated area and open it. Wipe down the inside of the chest with mineral spirits, which are available at a home-improvement or hardware store. *Follow directions exactly*. When totally dry, lightly sand the inside with 400-grit (very fine) sandpaper. Then vacuum up the shavings. You may have to repeat to eliminate the smell. Then you can apply cedar oil, available from cedar-chest manufacturers. The wood absorbs the oil, but be aware that the oil could stain items with which it comes in contact.

- All around the house: Have draperies, bedding and rugs professionally cleaned. If possible, place soft furnishing and other odor-absorbing items outside in the sun to air out. Open all windows and doors and turn on ceiling fans. The airing can take lots of time. You can mask the odor with air fresheners. In confined spaces, such as closets, put several bowls of activated charcoal (found at pet stores) around—out of the way of pets and children.

- Washable surfaces: Wipe down all hard surfaces with a solution of ½ cup vinegar and 1 quart water.

- Cars: If you've been storing an old car, get it out of the garage and into the sun! Open all the doors and windows. To get more air circulation, point a fan through the open doors. Be patient because it could take several days until the odor disappears. If the odor still persists, try an enzyme-based fabric spray sold for pet stains and odors.

MOUSE: A dead mouse or other small rodent can make one putrid odor! Vacuum or sweep the area completely, getting rid of any mouse remnants. (Be sure to wear gloves!) Then wipe down with a diluted solution of bleach or vinegar if safe for the surface. Place air fresheners or fabric-softener sheets in the area. Place a deodorizer near the air-conditioning intake or spray a room deodorizer on the air-conditioning filter and place the air-conditioning on fan. Repeat if needed!

NATURAL GAS ODOR: If you smell a leak:

1. Look for the source immediately—anything that runs on gas, such as the water heater or pilot lights on the stove.

2. Cut the gas supply and open all the windows so the gas leaves the house, particularly the kitchen.

Stinks

3. If you can't find the source and the gas odor remains, turn off the main gas valve and open the windows. CAUTION: Do not turn on anything, as an electric charge might cause an explosion. Do not use matches or candles. Leave the house ASAP and call the gas company from a neighbor's home.

FYI: Natural gas is odorless—therefore an additive is added, so if there is a leak, you will smell it.

OIL ODOR IN CAR: For temporary relief, put a scented fabric-softener sheet under a seat in the car to mask the smell. For the long-term, place a sock filled with activated charcoal inside the car. To eliminate odor from the cloth upholstery, clean well and spray with an enzyme-based fabric spray.

ONION ODOR ON HANDS: If you've sliced or peeled onions and your hands stink, try one or more of these methods:

- Dampen hands with water and sprinkle with salt. Rub the salt in and rinse.

- Wet your hands. Fill one palm with baking soda and rub well with the other. Rinse with warm water.

- Cover the smelly area with toothpaste or mouthwash. Rinse in warm water.

- Rub your hands with the dull side of a stainless-steel knife or stainless-steel kitchen sink.

OVEN-CLEANER ODOR: Remove the smelly residue leftover from oven cleaning with these three simple steps:

1. When you've finished cleaning the oven, place a layer of newspapers on the bottom of the oven.

2. Spray warm water on the top and side walls of the oven.

3. Use a clean cloth to dry the oven walls then discard the newspaper.

OVEN SPILLS: Baking food inevitably spills over in the oven. Sprinkle salt on the burned gunk. It will help to eliminate smoke, odors and make it easier to clean up after baking. To prevent spills, put a baking sheet or aluminum foil under things that contain foods that may bubble over or onto the bottom of the oven.

PAINT ODORS: To remove paint odor, try these methods:

- Turn on exhaust fans in kitchen or ceiling fans elsewhere. Open windows and doors in the rest of the house.

- Add a couple drops of vanilla to a gallon of paint. (If the paint is white or ivory, use one drop of lemon extract per gallon.)

- Cut large onions in half and place in the corners of a newly painted room.

- Set out several small bowls of vinegar around the room.

Stinks

PERSPIRATION ODOR IN CLOTHING: (See ANTIPERSPIRANT/ DEODORANT in Part Three: CLOTHING STAINS section.)

PILLOWS: To remove odors and freshen pillows first check the content and care labels. Before laundering, be sure to examine seams to make sure they're secure.

- Down: Wash in the washing machine, only two at a time on gentle cycle, agitating for only about 1 to 2 minutes. Toss a clean tennis ball into the dryer with the pillows, which helps plump them up, and add a fabric-softener sheet for a fresh fragrance.

- Foam: Wash by hand in a large bathtub or sink. Use a mild detergent and warm water. Air-dry them because foam could crumble in the dryer.

- Polyester: Follow same procedure as with down, above. These will not need as much time in the dryer.

For a quick refreshening, put bed pillows into the dryer on the air cycle with a fabric-softener sheet for around 20 minutes to fluff.

PLASTIC FOOD STORAGE CONTAINERS: To remove smells, fill the container with a solution of 1 tablespoon baking soda to 1 quart water, or soak small containers in a bucket or sink full of the solution. Let sit, then rinse with clean water and dry.

PLASTIC SHOWER CURTAIN: To get rid of the smell, put curtain into the dryer with a fabric-softener sheet on the air fluff cycle for several minutes.

PLASTIC TABLECLOTH: If your plastic tablecloth is smelly, soak or wash it in a solution of 1 tablespoon baking soda to 1 gallon of water. Rinse and hang to dry outside.

POTPOURRI: Heloise wet formula: Mix 2 cups rose petals, 2 cups rosemary, 2 cups mint, 4 cinnamon sticks, ½ cup whole allspice and 2 whole cloves. Put mixture in a large jar and cover with heated white vinegar. Allow the jar to sit for one week. To release the fragrance, simmer in a saucepan on low heat. (CAUTION: Watch carefully to make sure the pot doesn't go dry.) You can gather other flowers and spices to create your own special potpourri.

POTPOURRI (alternatives and substitutions): Make any area in your home smell wonderful with these methods:

- Simmer wet potpourri in a mug placed on a coffee-cup warmer.

- Microwave a bowl of potpourri and water. See CAUTION in POTPOURRI above.

POTPOURRI REFRESHENING: Add drops of your favorite perfume, perfume samples, or essential oils to jazz up old dry potpourri. Stir carefully and do not get any onto wood or laminate surfaces because it can stain.

POTTY CHAIR: To deodorize a potty chair during training time, sprinkle baking soda under the bowl of the potty chair to help eliminate any lingering smells.

Stinks

REFRIGERATOR (meat spoilage): Remove everything from both the refrigerator and freezer compartments. Sprinkle baking soda on a damp sponge (or mix 1 cup ammonia with 1 gallon water) and wipe the inside completely, including baskets, racks and underneath vegetable bins. Be sure to check the drip pan for any blood that might have leaked down. After the refrigerator is clean, place a dish of vanilla or lemon extract or an opened box of baking soda inside or pour dry unused coffee grounds onto several paper plates. Set them on separate shelves. It may take several days for the odor to dissipate.

REFRIGERATOR DEODORIZER: These tried-and-true methods work:

- Put a box of baking soda into the refrigerator or put the baking soda into a plastic margarine tub and poke several holes in the lid and change it at least every 3 months. When you do, pour it down the sink to freshen it or pour it on a wet sponge and wipe out the inside of the refrigerator for extra cleaning. (Note: Do not recycle the baking soda from the refrigerator for use in recipes because the absorbed odors would be transferred to the food.)

- Place lemon or lime slices on small dishes and put on different shelves.

- Wipe out refrigerator walls with white household vinegar.

- If you are moving or putting a refrigerator in storage for a short time, place socks filled with dry coffee grounds or activated charcoal to prevent musty odors.

Heloise Conquers Stinks and Stains

RODENT CAGES: To deodorize a hamster or gerbil "aquarium," first empty the aquarium of everything—bedding, toys, and animals—and put it into the shower. Fill with a half-inch or so of water and a couple of tablespoons of baking soda. Scrub the bottom and sides. Rinse with clear water. The smells will be gone and the glass will sparkle.

ROOM DEODORIZER: To make an aromatic pomander ball, make holes in the skin of an orange with a round toothpick then push cloves into the holes. Cover the orange completely or make a design. Wrap with a ribbon and hang.

ROOM DEODORIZER (mushrooms): To renew the scent, place several drops of a liquid deodorizer or your favorite perfume on the top of the mushroom.

ROOM DEODORIZER (vacuuming): Put a scented fabric-softener sheet into the bag of your upright vacuum cleaner to create a fresh smell. This should last for several weeks.

ROOM FRAGRANCE FROM FIREPLACE: Toss a handful of fresh or dried herbs, spices or several cinnamon sticks on a small fire. Bags of scented chips also add a wonderful aroma.

RUBBER GLOVES: To prevent odor, sprinkle the inside of the gloves with baking soda or talcum powder. Or, dry the outside surface while you have them on; then pull them off turning them inside out; hang on a towel rack to air-dry.

Stinks

SHOES/SNEAKERS: Pour a bit of baking soda inside shoes and allow it to sit overnight. In the morning, pour the baking soda down the bathroom sink to recycle it. Use insole liners to absorb future odors. Also, spray with deodorant.

SILK FABRIC: According to our friends at The International Fabricare Institute, silk fabrics will have an odor if, during the manufacturing process, the fabric was not boiled properly and all the sericin or gum was not removed. There is really nothing you can do—even a dry cleaner cannot remove this odor without the possibility of color loss, fabric damage or shrinkage. If the silk is washable (read care label), use 1 teaspoon mild soap for each garment. Put into warm water and let soak for several minutes. Rinse thoroughly in warm water and air-dry. If smell still remains, take to a dry cleaner and have deodorized.

SKUNK (on dog): This is the worst smell! Some claim that rubbing tomato juice into the dog's fur and a good washing will do the trick. Alas, not so well. My vet and many others recommend this mixture to remove that awful odor: 1 quart 3-percent hydrogen peroxide, 1 cup baking soda, 1 teaspoon mild dishwashing liquid. Mix well and rub it through your dog's fur, just like shampoo. Don't let any get into your pet's eyes or ears. Rinse well with clear water.

SLEEPING BAG: Avoid musty odors by placing fabric-softener sheets in the bag before rolling it up for storage.

SMOKE: (See also CIGARETTE.)

- In clothes: Most can be removed by repeated washing. However, if the odor does not diminish, you can take clothes to a dry cleaner that has an ozone generator, which should do the job.

- In the home: Getting rid of an overwhelming smoke smell can be especially difficult because the two biggest areas that absorb odors are walls and flooring. First, a quick fix: If a room smells of smoke from a party or the fireplace, open the windows and doors to get it out. Then take a small tea towel and soak it in white household vinegar and water. Wring out to eliminate excess water and then swing it around the room.

- My mother would set out bowls of vinegar or ammonia to eliminate smoke odors. Place a couple around your rooms during the day and see if you notice a difference when you return at night. CAUTION: Don't use ammonia if you have pets or small children.

- For serious smoke smells, you'll have to clean the walls. If they can be "wet washed," use a nonabrasive, all-purpose cleaner. If the odor remains, you may have to repaint the walls, being sure to use a sealer first.

- If your rooms are carpeted, you can buy special cleaners that can help remove the smoke: dry carpet cleaner with granules that are brushed into the carpet and then vacuumed up; deodorizing cleaners that are sprinkled onto the carpet and vacuumed up; carpet cleaning machines that use detergent and water solutions. As a last resort, call the professionals! (See Part Four: CARPET STAINS section.)

Stinks

SOCKS: For particularly smelly socks, wash as usual, then rinse in a solution of ¼ cup white vinegar to 1 gallon water. Let them soak for a bit and squeeze out excess water. Do not rinse again. Then dry.

STUFFED TOY DEODORIZING: To clean nonwashable stuffed toys, put the toy in a big plastic bag with a ½ cup of baking soda. Close the top securely and then shake, shake, shake. Go outside to remove the stuffed toy and again shake well to remove the rest of the baking soda. Use a soft hairbrush to eliminate any remaining baking soda.

SUEDE: New suede can have an overwhelming odor, most likely as a result of the manufacturing process. Hang the garment outside to air or have it "flushed" out by a professional leather cleaner.

TOASTER OVEN: To help contain the smell of burnt crumbs and grease, pour a bit of baking soda on the bottom tray. Be sure to clean the tray as often as possible to prevent a fire.

TOBACCO SMOKE: See SMOKE and CIGARETTE.

TOILET BOWL: To deodorize, pour a cup or so of undiluted white vinegar into the bowl, and let stand for about 5 minutes. Scrub and then flush.

TOOLBOX: To eliminate odors, take out all tools. Clean the box with an all-purpose cleaner and let dry completely. Wipe all tools with a clean, dry cloth. To help keep the box fresh, put baking soda in a clean, plastic margarine tub with several holes poked in the lid.

TOWELS: To get rid of the sour smell, wash towels in small loads, using hot water, the normal amount of detergent plus ½ cup baking soda or 1 cup ammonia to the rinse cycle. Put into dryer right away. You may have to wash several times. Between washes, it's not a bad idea to give damp towels a few tumbles in the dryer.

TRASH COMPACTOR: Boy, odors can grow in this handy kitchen appliance. Before you put any trash into the bag, place a thick layer of newspaper on the bottom and cover it with a layer of baking soda. As trash accumulates, keep it odor-free by tossing a handful of baking soda on top.

URINE:

- In carpets: First you must soak up as much of the urine residue ASAP. Use several layers of paper towel or a thick old cloth, and stomp on it to absorb moisture. Be sure to check the padding underneath where the urine may have soaked through. (See PET STAINS in Part Four: CARPET STAINS section.) After urine has been completely removed and dried thoroughly, you can sprinkle baking soda over the DRIED area or place a fabric-softener sheet between the carpet and the underpadding to mask any lingering odor.

Stinks

- In clothing: In baby, children's and adult clothing, these odors (and stains) can be tough to remove. If you can get to the clothing immediately, it will be easier to deal with the problem, because the stain will not set into the fabric. First, soak the items in water (see note below) and then wash in the hottest water possible that's safe for the fabric. Read the care labels and follow instructions precisely. (For more specific instructions, see URINE in Part Three: CLOTHING STAINS section.)

After washing, line drying or airing the clothes in the sun will help to eliminate smells. Super-strength commercial cleaning formulas are geared specifically to removing urine odor. However, removal may take several applications. Many of my readers highly recommend enzyme-based products that remove pet-urine odors and stains, which are available at pet stores. You may want to try them on people odors and stains, too.

VACUUM CLEANER BAG: Any of the following, added to the bag, will eliminate that musty, dusty vacuum cleaner "exhaust": Carpet freshener, several whole cloves, baking soda, a cotton ball dabbed with almond or peppermint extract or your favorite perfume.

WASHING MACHINE HOSES AND DRAINS: To freshen, pour a cup of white vinegar and run a small-load cycle.

WASHING MACHINE ODOR: Follow these steps:

1. Turn water-level dial to the highest setting.

2. Set the water-temperature dial to hot and fill washer tub.

3. Set wash on normal wash and start cycle.

4. Stop after 1 minute. Add a gallon more of hot water. Do not let tub overflow.

5. Add 2 to 4 cups household chlorine bleach.

6. Begin cycle again and allow to run for several minutes, then stop and let sit for 15 to 30 minutes.

7. Turn on and let washing machine complete rest of cycle. When completed, open lid and allow the drum to air out. Also, leave the lid open when not in use.

WASTEBASKET: To prevent odors, put a fabric-softener sheet or perfume strips or samples into the bottom of the basket.

WATERBED: If you determine that the plastic covering is the cause of odors, wash it with a mixture of baking soda and water. However, if bacteria are growing in the water inside the mattress, get a commercial product at a waterbed shop.

WORKSHOP: Place several containers filled with baking soda around the work area. To prevent spills, used lidded containers with holes punched in the tops.

Stinks

PART TWO

Stains

Lady Liberty Cleaned Up!

Did you know that the interior walls of the Statue of Liberty were cleaned with baking soda? About 200 tons of it was blasted from a spray gun to get rid of 99 years of paint and coal tar. Baking soda was used because it wouldn't hurt the copper! The cleaning of the Statue of Liberty may not have been the biggest cleaning job in the world, but it is certainly a testament to a Heloise favorite cleaner/deodorizer. Along with vinegar, I probably recommend baking soda more often than any other products—homemade or commercial.

I believe that there's usually a remedy for every stain. Some might demand a little bit of imagination. Others will need a lot of patience. And, you'll even see in these pages an entry called "When All Else Fails," which asks you to accept the inevitable . . . the stain will always be with you but you can learn to live with the stain—or sew on a patch to hide it. Be as creative as you can.

The best way to conquer any stain is to have knowledge and a plan. In the following pages I'll give you tried-and-true stain removal guidelines, information about types of stains and the kinds of cleaners plus a host of invaluable, home-tested hints and tips. If the solution to your problem isn't in the pages of this book, I hope that you will contact me at the address or e-mail provided and share your favorite stain stories. Perhaps we can find the solution together or another reader will have found the remedy that we can pass on. (Contact me by fax at 1-210-HELOISE or visit my my website at www.Heloise.com.)

The 3 Rules: Soon, Slow, Several!

Always keep these rules in mind when you take on any stain.

1. As SOON as possible—ASAP. Attack the stain as SOON as you can. The more time left on the fabric, the more difficult it will be to remove!

2. Lift the stain SLOWLY. Some stains take time to get out.

3. Repeat these steps for stubborn stains. You may have to do them SEVERAL times.

8 Steps to Effective Stain Removal

Sometimes it just takes one quick step to get the stain out. Sometimes you need to be more diligent and patient.

1. Read First, Act Later—but not too late: Read the care label and follow the instructions precisely.

2. Gentle to Hard: Trying the least drastic stain removal first may do the job.

3. Flush: Flush or soak the stained areas ASAP with cold water. Many times this gentlest of methods will remove the stain. But watch for delicate fabrics that may be damaged by water.

4. Protect and Absorb: Placing a paper towel—or several layers to be extra safe—underneath a stain before treating will absorb any stain that's going through the fabric.

5. From the outside in: Work from the outside toward the center of the stain to prevent it from spreading.

6. Blot, don't rub: Except where otherwise instructed, BLOTTING—dabbing firmly with an absorbent cloth—is better than RUBBING—using a circular motion to gently scrub the area. Be aware that rubbing may spread the stain and damage the fabric.

7. Time heals all: Give your stain remover enough time to work before rinsing or washing. Don't rush it or you may have to repeat it.

8. This is a test: Always test a small hidden area first just in case your cleaning method proves to be as damaging as the stain. This is especially important if you don't know what the fabric is.

What Kind of Stain Is That, Anyway?

It's key to know what kind of a stain you have in order to treat it properly and with the right product. Here are the three basic types you need to know:

GREASE AND OIL: Butter, candle wax, chocolate and crayon are a few of the major culprits that cause these stains. Washables are best treated with warm or hot water. But remember that many greasy food stains also contain protein and/or sugar.

PROTEIN: Baby formula, blood, cheese, egg, ice cream, urine, yogurt and grass. Use cold water to wash blood- or egg-stained items; and cool to warm for other stains of this kind.

SUGAR: Since sugar hides in so many foods from fruit and juices to chocolate, you have to be careful because heat may set sugar stains. A greasy stain may require hot water but a sugar stain should be treated with cool water first.

The Right Cleaner for the Job

There are a wide variety of cleaners available: both commercial products and money saving homemade remedies. Since any of these can be used for stains on clothes, carpets, or anywhere around the house, you might want to have all or most of these on hand.

ACETONE: This highly flammable, colorless liquid is used to dissolve fats, oils and waxes.

AMMONIA: Cuts heavy soil and grease when added with detergent. CAUTION: DO NOT EVER combine ammonia with chlorine bleach or products containing chlorine bleach because mixed together they create hazardous fumes.

BAR SOAP: Bathroom and laundry bar soaps and powders can be used to pretreat serious stains or soiling before laundering. They can be helpful when you need to wash hand-washable lingerie. Bars do a good job removing perspiration and tobacco stains.

BORAX: Boosts laundry cleaning. (Available in the detergent section of your supermarket.)

CHLORINE BLEACH: Apply this ONLY to white clothing unless diluted to the correct solution per instructions on the bottle. Read and follow the clothing care labels. DO NOT put on acetates, silk, spandex, wool or some flame-retardant fabrics.

CLEANING SOLVENT (dry-cleaning fluid): Removes cosmetics, grease and gum stains. Use also on dry-cleanable clothing.

DETERGENTS: Liquid detergents can be used to pretreat stains and perform more effectively than powdered no-phosphate detergents. However, powdered phosphate detergents (they are banned in some areas) do work in soft and hard water. Powders are effective on ground-in dirt and clay. Liquids are good for food, grease and oil stains.

ENZYMES: These proteins are used in laundry products because they break up protein-type stains as mentioned above (blood, chocolate, egg, meat juice, baby formula, grass, dairy products, body fluids). Check the label of presoak and regular detergents because some contain enzymes, and look at laundry detergent labels, too. If you are not clear, call the manufacturer's 800-number on the package.

HYDROGEN PEROXIDE (3 percent): As a mild, slow-acting oxidizing bleach, it lifts bloodstains and whitens lace.

ISOAMYL ACETATE: Called banana or pear oil, it dissolves paint and lacquer.

OXALIC ACID CRYSTALS: Used for bleaching and cleaning.

OXYGEN BLEACH: Applies to all types of colors and fabric. The powdered version provides detergent and an all-fabric bleaching action good for stain and soil removal.

PART THREE

Where do these stains on our clothing come from? Thin air it seems! When we're at work or play, we suddenly notice a spot or stain. To most of us, they are mystery stains. I like to think of myself as the Stain Detective. And, I hope that with the help of this book you, too, can become the Sherlock Holmes or Nancy Drew of the stain world.

Like any good detective, you need to understand everything about the perpetrator and the victim. The major types of stains first appeared on page 44 in the general introduction to stains, but I repeat them here for your convenience:

Types of Stains

GREASE AND OIL: Butter, candle wax, chocolate and crayon are a few of the major culprits that cause these stains. Washables are best treated with warm or hot water. But remember that many greasy food stains also contain protein and/or sugar.

PROTEIN: Baby formula, blood, cheese, egg, ice cream, urine, yogurt and grass. Use cold water to wash blood- or egg-stained items; and cool to warm for other stains of this kind.

SUGAR: Since sugar hides in so many foods, from fruit and juices to chocolate, you have to be careful because heat may set sugar stains. A greasy stain may require hot water but a sugar stain should be treated with cool water first.

Fabrics: A Stain Fighter's Glossary

Knowing the rules for stain removal, understanding the major types of stains that can cause you grief, and learning about the types of cleaners that are available are the first three parts of your education in effective stain removal. It is equally important to know the types and styles of fabrics that you are trying to clean since so much depends on it. But be sure to always read the care instructions if they are attached to the item. If not, you'll have to figure out what kind of fabric you are working with and consult the following list from the International Fabricare Institute:

ACETATE: A synthetic fiber that is used for luxurious fabrics such as taffeta and satin. It is often blended with rayon.

ACRYLIC: The generic name for a synthetic fiber derived from polyacrylonitrile. Acrylic is typically used as a substitute for wool.

ANGORA: A hair (wool) fiber from the Angora rabbit. It may be blended with rayon or wool fibers for a novelty effect.

ARAMID: A generic name for a synthetic fiber that is very strong and highly flame-resistant. Trade names are Nomex and Kevlar.

BIAS: The diagonal of a woven fabric between the warp and the filling (crosswire) threads. This part of the fabric has the greatest amount of stretch and can easily be distorted in the cleaning and pressing process.

BLEEDING: The running of dyes that aren't colorfast in solvent or water. When the color runs it can stain other materials.

BLEND: A fabric made from two or more fibers that will have the performance characteristics of both fibers (i.e., a cotton and blend).

BOUCLE: A rough, fairly thick, stubborn yarn that gives a fabric a tufted or knotted texture.

BROCADE: A heavy jacquard weave fabric with a design, such as leaves and flowers, woven into it. Metallic threads are often used in brocades.

BUGLE BEADS: Tube-shaped beads, originally made of glass although often man-made. They are sewn on dresses and blouses

Clothing

as decoration. These beads may contain a coating on the inside that can be removed in dry cleaning, giving the bead a translucent appearance, or can discolor during long-term storage.

CASHMERE: A fine, soft wool obtained from goats native to Kashmir and Tibet.

CELLULOSE: Fibers that come from a plant source, such as cotton, linen, ramie, and rayon.

CHENILLE: From the French word for caterpillar, a fuzzy pile yarn that resembles a caterpillar or pipe cleaner. Commonly found in rugs, bedspreads, and bathroom accessories, but also used in sweaters, blouses, and dresses.

CHIFFON: A sheer, lightweight, drapable, woven fabric originally made of silk but today usually made from man-made fibers.

CHINTZ: Any closely woven, plain weave fabric with a shiny lustrous finish, often printed in bright floral designs.

COLORFAST: A term that implies that the color in a fabric will not be removed in the recommended cleaning procedure and will not wash out or fade upon exposure to sunlight or other atmospheric elements.

CORDUROY: A pile-corded fabric in which the rib has been sheared or woven to produce a smooth, velvet-like nap.

CREPE: A fabric with an overall crinkled surface that is made from yarns with such a high twist that the yarn actually kinks.

DENIM: A twill weave fabric with a colored warp and white filling thread.

FAILLE: A woven fabric that has a very narrow, crosswire rib.

FAKE (FUN) FUR: A common term for synthetic fabrics used to imitate animal pelts.

FELT: A fabric made from wool, fur, or hair fibers that mesh together when heat, moisture, and mechanical action are applied.

FLOCKING: A term used to describe small pieces of fiber glued or bonded to the surface of a fabric.

FUSIBLE: A fabric with an adhesive coating that can be attached to another fabric by applying heat, moisture and pressure.

INTERFACING: A fabric used to give additional body and strength to certain parts of garments. Some areas that usually contain interfacing include front opening edges, collars, and pocket flaps. Some interfacing material may not be compatible with the shell fabric and may cause a bubbling or puckering of the shell fabric.

JERSEY: A single-knit fabric with plain stitches on the right side and purl stitches on the back. The word *jersey* is often used to describe any knit.

Clothing

KNIT: A method of making fabrics through the interlacing of yarns. These fabrics tend to mold and fit body shapes and are marked by their ability to stretch and recover to the original size.

LACE: Knotted, twisted or looped yarns that produce a fragile, sheer fabric, usually with intricate design patterns.

METALLICS: Man-made mineral fibers composed of metal, plastic-coated metal, metal-coated plastic, or a core completely covered with metal. Metallic fibers are primarily used to create shiny, decorative yarns.

NAP: A fuzzy or soft downlike surface produced by brushing the fabric, usually with wire brushes.

NON-WOVEN: Fabrics made from fibers that are held together in a web by mechanical or chemical means or through heat. Some examples include felt and Ultrasuede.

OXFORD: A fabric woven in a basket weave and made of cotton or a cotton blend. It often has a thin, colored warp and a thick, white filling.

PILE: A woven fabric containing an extra set of yarns woven into the base of the fabric to produce the hairlike surface texture. Velvet, velveteen, corduroy, and fake fur are the most common pile fabrics.

PILLING: The tendency of fibers to pill or roll up. Pilling occurs when the loose end of a fiber is rubbed and collected on the surface of the fabric. The length of the fiber and twist of the yarn will affect pilling.

RAYON: The generic name for a cellulose-based, man-made fiber. Rayon has characteristics similar to those of cotton, linen, and ramie.

SATIN: Fabrics that are characterized by yarns that usually float over four to seven yarns before being interlaced with yarns laid in the opposite direction. The floating yarns along the surface reflect light, which gives the fabric its luster. Satin fabrics can be made from silk or man-made fibers like acetate or polyester.

SHELL: The outer fabric of a garment or household item.

SILK: A natural filament fiber produced by silkworms when spinning their cocoons.

SIZING: A term for materials used to give a fabric stiffness, luster, or firmness. Different types of material are used on different fabrics.

VELVET: A fabric with a short, closely woven pile. It is usually made of rayon, acetate, silk, nylon, or a blend of these fibers.

WEAVE: Yarns interlacing at right angles. There are three basic weave types: plain, twill, and satin. All other weaves are variations of these. Some of the more common variations include basket, rib and jacquard.

Clothing

WOOLEN: A wool fabric made from loosely twisted yarns that has a somewhat fuzzy surface.

WORSTED: A wool fabric with a clean, smooth surface made from tightly twisted yarns.

YARN: A continuous strand spun from short (staple) fibers or long (filament) fibers. Yarns can be of low twist (lofty) or high twist (tight).

Laundry Products: A Primer

Knowing the different products and their ingredients helps you select the right product for the cleaning job. The following list, courtesy of The Soap and Detergent Association, gives you the general types of cleaners available. (See also Cleaners in the introduction to the STAINS section on page 45.)

Overflow!

Have you ever added too much soap to the washing machine and suddenly suds are flowing out everywhere? Grab a saltshaker and sprinkle salt on the suds; they will dissipate immediately.

LAUNDRY DETERGENTS and **LAUNDRY AIDS** are available as liquids, powders, gels, sticks, sprays, pumps, sheets and bars. They are formulated to meet a variety of soil and stain removal, bleaching, fabric softening and conditioning, and disinfectant needs under varying water, temperature and use conditions.

LAUNDRY DETERGENTS are either general purpose or light-duty. General-purpose detergents are suitable for all washable fabrics. Liquids work best on oily stains and for pretreating soils and stains. Powders are especially effective in lifting out clay and ground-in dirt. Light-duty detergents are used for hand- or machine-washing lightly soiled items and delicate fabrics.

LAUNDRY AIDS contribute to the effectiveness of laundry detergents and provide special functions.

BLEACHES (chlorine and oxygen) whiten and brighten fabrics and help remove stubborn stains. They convert soils into colorless, soluble particles that can be removed by detergents and carried away in the wash water. Liquid chlorine bleach (usually in a sodium hypochlorite solution) can also disinfect and deodorize fabrics. Oxygen (color-safe) bleach is gentler and works safely on almost all washable fabrics.

BLUINGS contain a blue dye or pigment taken up by fabrics in the wash or rinse. Bluing absorbs the yellow part of the light spectrum, counteracting the natural yellowing of many fabrics.

BOOSTERS enhance the soil and stain removal, brightening, buffering and water softening performance of detergents. They are used in the wash in addition to the detergent.

ENYZYME PRESOAKS are used for soaking items before washing to remove difficult stains and soils. When added to the wash water, they increase cleaning power.

Clothing

FABRIC SOFTENERS, added to the final rinse or dryer, make fabrics softer and fluffier; decrease static cling, wrinkling and drying time; impart a pleasing fragrance and make ironing easier.

PREWASH SOIL AND STAIN REMOVERES are used to pretreat heavily soiled and stained garments, especially those made from synthetic fibers.

Heloise Make-Your-Own Prewash Spray

Mix equal parts of regular (not concentrated) hand dishwashing (NOT dishwasher) liquid, household ammonia and water. Pour into a clean spray bottle and label clearly. Store away from the reach of children and pets. When you use it on a stain, wash the garment immediately!

STARCHES, FABRIC FINISHES AND SIZINGS used in the final rinse or after drying give body to fabrics, make them more soil-resistant and make ironing easier.

WATER SOFTENERS added to the wash or rinse, inactivate hard-water minerals. Since detergents are more effective in soft water, these products increase cleaning power.

A Shopping List of Laundry Supplies

Many of the items listed below were explained in the general introduction to stains but here's a quick checklist of the laundry supplies you might want to have on hand.

Ammonia

Baking Soda

Bleaches:
Chlorine and oxygen
Dishwasher powder or liquid
Fabric color remover; or substitutes such as lemon juice

Club soda

Detergents:
enzymes and presoaks
heavy-duty powder
liquid and light-duty liquid for delicates

Cleaning fluids:
amyl acetate or acetone, an odorless, fragrance-free ingredient in nail polish remover
dry-cleaning solvent/fluid
nail polish remover
rubbing alcohol

Glycerin

Oxalic acid

Rust-stain remover

Spot-and-stain remover

White bar soap

White vinegar

Clothing

20 Nifty Laundry Tricks and Tips

1. Establish the household rule that all family members have to let you know about clothing spots and stains, so you can pretreat. Have family members loosely tie part of the leg or shirtsleeve as a marker that the item has a spot, or they do their own laundry.

2. Make laundry sorting easier for your children by giving each one a different colored laundry basket to keep in their room. After laundering, you can put the clean clothes in the right basket and they can take it to their rooms to put away.

3. Close all zippers and hook all fasteners before you put them into the washing machine or dryer because otherwise they will snag and possibly get bent or broken.

4. Sew on loose buttons; repair rips and tears before putting into the washing machine or dryer.

5. Check pockets to remove all items before putting into the washing machine.

6. Turn jeans, corduroys, or velveteens inside out when you wash them so they won't fade. Wash in the coolest water and dry on the lowest heat.

7. Wash and dry printed T-shirts and sweaters inside-out to prevent pilling.

8. Read and follow the care label and manufacturer's instructions when caring for rayon or rayon-blend fabrics.

Most can be machine-washed and tumble-dried but will shrink unless a preshrinking finish has been applied.

9. If you need to use a spray-type laundry stain remover, be sure to turn the stained item inside-out and spray the stain from the back side.

10. Rub a small bit of liquid detergent on stained polyester garments before putting into the washing machine.

11. Test a garment for colorfastness by making a solution of 1 tablespoon 5 percent bleach and ¼ cup water. Using an inside seam, put a drop or two of the solution on it for just 1 minute to see if color changes. Then rinse and air-dry.

12. Wash same-colored clothing together to avoid fading and bleeding.

13. Do not use chlorine or non-chlorine bleaches together.

14. Use the right water temperature; otherwise you can damage more delicate washables.

15. Never overload the washing machine because clothes won't get clean.

16. Do not put wet colored garments into a laundry hamper with white garments; they could bleed color onto them.

17. Remove lint from the dryer filter after dryer load. Clothes will dry faster and energy will be saved, too.

18. Never overload the dryer since it adds to drying time and your clothes will come out wrinkled.

Clothing

19. Do not add wet garments to the dryer with a partially dried load.

20. Don't dry some of the "newer" white fabrics in natural sunlight because they contain fluorescent brighteners, which react in the sun and may cause fabric to become yellowed permanently.

Clothing Stains A-to-Z

ACETATE (triacetate): Check the label to find out if the item needs to be dry-cleaned. If not, wash in warm water in a washing machine on the gentle cycle. Never twist or ring when wet. Use fabric softener to reduce static electricity. Always iron on a low setting or use steam.

ACNE MEDICATIONS/SKIN CREAMS: These may contain bleaches, like benzoyl peroxide, which can discolor fabrics. Let medications dry completely after applying and before putting on clothing. Wash hands well and dry completely after applying so none will get onto clothing. If it does, the stain or discoloration may be permanent.

ACRYLIC: Use warm water in machine washing and tumble dry.

ADHESIVE TAPE: Apply ice or freeze the sticky residue by putting the garment into the freezer. With a dull knife blade, carefully scrape off the hardened gummy residue. Pretreat area with a petroleum-based prewash spray and launder as usual.

ALCOHOLIC BEVERAGES: Use cool water to soak or sponge the stain immediately. Then pour a bit of white household vinegar on a sponge and apply to the stain. Rinse. If any stain remains, gently rub liquid laundry detergent into it, then launder as usual. (See also WINE.)

ANTIPERSPIRANT/DEODORANT: Salts from perspiration can eat away at fabrics. (Antiperspirants that contain aluminum chloride can cause fabrics like rayon to turn yellow.)

When these stains happen, get to them ASAP. CAUTION: Ironing may set the stains.

- *Fresh and light stain:* Rub liquid laundry detergent or pre-wash stain remover into the stained area. Use the hottest water safe for the fabric and wash. If stains remain, apply white household vinegar and let sit for 30 minutes. Then wash the garment using an enzyme detergent or oxygen bleach.

- *Heavy stain:* Place the stain facedown on a paper towel and sponge the back of the stain (outside of garment) with a dry-cleaning solvent. Let dry and rinse. Rub in liquid laundry detergent and launder in the hottest water safe for the fabric.

- *Older stain:* Apply undiluted white vinegar, rinse and launder as usual.

- *To help prevent stains,* let deodorant dry completely before you dress.

Clothing

- *To prevent buildup*, do not wash garments repeatedly in cold water because it may not break down the deodorant or perspiration buildup, but be sure to:
  - Wash the clothing after every wearing and don't put it away without cleaning.
  - Rub liquid laundry detergent onto the underarm area of the garment, and after every third or fourth wearing use the hottest water safe for the material.

ARTIST'S OILS: While turpentine will remove oil paint, it also will discolor some fabric. Use bar face soap to remove artist's oil paint from clothing.

Note: Bar soap can also be used to clean brushes. Apply soap and brush under warm running water. Rub the brush into the soap, moving from side-to-side. With your fingers rub soap through the bristles until paint is gone. Rinse with clear warm water.

BABY FORMULA: Soak clothes in cold water ASAP, and then rub liquid laundry detergent into the stain or treat with an enzyme presoak or prewash spray. Launder in the hottest water safe for the fabric. If the stain persists, sponge it with dry-cleaning fluid and launder a second time before putting into the dryer.

As a last-ditch try for white, chlorine-bleachable clothing, use a large non-aluminum container or your kitchen sink. Fill with 1 gallon hot water, add ½ cup dishwasher detergent and ¼ cup bleach and NOTHING else. Stir until detergent is dissolved.

Add clothes and let soak for 15 minutes or a little longer if still stained. For fabrics that can't be washed in hot water, such as nylon, let mixture cool before placing clothes into it. Note: If

Heloise's Last-Resort Stain Remover

First printed in my mother's newspaper column more than 40 years ago, this is my favorite last-ditch stain remover. It can be used for white and bleachable clothes, but not for silk or rayon. Here's how to make it:

1 gallon hot water
1 cup powdered dishwasher detergent
¼ cup household liquid chlorine bleach

Mix completely in a plastic, enamel or stainless-steel container, as it will discolor aluminum ones.

Let garment soak in the mixture for 5 to 10 minutes. If any of the stain is still visible, soak the garment a little longer. Then wash as usual.

formula stains are left to set, they will become permanent and no amount of bleach will remove them!

BASEBALL CAPS: Test cap for colorfastness first by using a small amount of detergent and water on a hidden spot. Blot area with a white cloth. If any dye comes off on the cloth, it might not be a good idea to try to clean it. If dye does not come off, hand wash with laundry detergent, rinse and air-dry. To clean the sweatband, use the kind of spot remover that you spray on that dries to a powder. Follow directions carefully. Use a clean toothbrush to brush off powder. Or, put a small amount of this homestyle solution using 1 tablespoon hair shampoo to ½ cup of water onto the band; scrub it in with the toothbrush. Rinse carefully and let air-dry.

Clothing

Baseball cap forms are available in sporting good stores and they will help keep the shape of the cap when drying. Putting caps into the dishwasher or washing machine could damage the brim.

BEER: Rinse with cool water, then sponge stains with white household vinegar.

BERRY: See FRUIT/FRUIT JUICE/BERRIES.

BLANKETS (cotton, rayon, or other synthetics): For heavily stained or soiled blankets, prespot and presoak. Wash 4 to 6 minutes in cold or warm water (depending on the care label) on the delicate cycle with detergent and an oxygen bleach (if label says okay). Dry on gentle cycle or line dry. For a quick freshening, put into dryer on air setting with a fabric softener sheet.

BLOOD: Treat the stain ASAP. Do not use hot water because heat may set protein stains.

- Get the stained item into cold water and soak for 30 minutes. Then apply a prewash stain remover. If stain remains, rub it with liquid laundry detergent or bar soap. Still a problem? Make a solution of 1 tablespoon ammonia and 1 cup water and apply to the stains. Rinse and launder following care-label instructions. Check garment before putting into dryer. If the stain is still there, pour a small amount of 3 percent hydrogen peroxide on the stain (always test this on a hidden area to see if the 3 percent hydrogen peroxide affects fabric color). Launder again.

- Unseasoned meat tenderizer is also effective in getting rid of fresh bloodstains. Dampen the area with cold water then sprinkle on unseasoned meat tenderizer and let sit. Repeat to remove all of the stain; then the garment can be laundered.

If stain has dried, soak in warm water with an enzyme-based product. Then launder as usual.

BREAST MILK: Soak clothes in cold water ASAP, and then rub liquid laundry detergent into the stain or treat with an enzyme presoak or prewash spray. Launder in the hottest water safe for the fabric. If the stain persists, sponge it with dry-cleaning fluid and launder a second time before putting into the dryer.

> ### When All Else Fails!
>
> *In spite of your best efforts, some stains are permanent. But you can get around that by sewing or ironing on an appliqué design patch over that hopeless stain or scorch mark. It just may be your fashion statement!*

BUTTER/MARGARINE: For washable fabrics, pretreat with a heavy-duty liquid laundry detergent or a prewash spray. Then launder as usual. For heavy stains on washable fabrics, put stained areas facedown on paper towels. Apply dry-cleaning solvent to the backside of the stain; replace towels frequently. Let dry; rub in liquid detergent. Rinse and launder. Nonwashables need to be professionally dry-cleaned.

If you're out and about and spill grease or oil on your favorite article, don't fret. Simply pat on some flour, talc or even white artificial sugar onto the grease spot. When absorbed, brush off and then wash or take to the cleaners as soon as possible. It may be necessary to pretreat with a stain remover and wash in the hottest water safe for the fabric.

CANDLE WAX: Use a plastic card or your fingernail to lift off as much of the wax as you can. (Even the dull side of a knife may damage certain fabrics so do this step with care.) Then, put paper towels on each side of the stained area. Use an iron, turned to a low-to-medium setting, depending on what's appropriate for the fabric. Check the care labels on the fabrics and your iron to determine the temperature. For example, linen and cotton can tolerate high temperatures better than polyester or other synthetic fabrics. Press the stained area until wax comes up and replace the towels often to absorb it. If there's still a stain, make a mixture of 1 tablespoon mild white dishwashing liquid, 1 teaspoon household ammonia and 1 cup of water and treat it. Then wash in the hottest water safe for the fabric (check the care label). Or, to remove the stain, you can apply full-strength liquid laundry detergent, allowing it to set, then washing as usual.

CANDY (other than chocolate): Use cold water and a small amount of liquid detergent on the stain; then rinse. If the stains are red, soak the garment in a strong laundry detergent and a bit of bleach (if it's okay for the material) or apply a prewash spray.

CARBON PAPER: Dampen area and rub liquid laundry detergent into the stain. Hand wash garment in warm, soapy water. Rinse and repeat steps if needed.

CHEESE: As soon as possible, soak clothes in cold water and then rub liquid laundry detergent into the stain or treat with an enzyme presoak or prewash spray. Launder in the hottest water safe for the fabric. If the stain persists, sponge it with dry-cleaning fluid and launder a second time before putting into the dryer.

CHEWING GUM: Put the garment in the freezer to harden the gum. CAUTION: Don't put the garment into a plastic bag. Then remove residue by scraping very carefully with a dull knife or credit card. If you still see residue, sponge dry-cleaning fluid on the area or treat with prewash spray and then launder.

CHOCOLATE: Scrape away any chocolate you can. Try these methods: Soak the garment in cold water for 30 minutes. While the fabric is wet, rub liquid laundry detergent into the stain. Rinse. If a greasy stain remains, sponge it with dry-cleaning fluid. Rinse. Launder in warm water.

Or: Blot the spot with cool water. Then presoak with a powdered laundry detergent with enzymes. Follow the label directions. Launder as usual.

Treat with a solution of 1 teaspoon household ammonia diluted in 1 cup water.

(CAUTION: Do NOT use this on wool or silk blends). Launder as usual.

CHRISTENING GOWN: When you buy the gown, check the care label to know in advance how the dress can be cleaned. A gown decorated with lace or pearls may be difficult to clean at home and most likely need to be professionally cleaned. As soon as possible after the christening, take the dress to be dry-cleaned by a professional—even if it looks clean! It may have spots from the baby, which you can't see. There also could be stains that will oxidize and show up as brown/yellow spots later.

CLAY: Sports or gardening stains of this nature can be difficult to remove but give this a shot. First, eliminate any dry dirt; shake or brush off. Combine powdered detergent (that contains no bleach) and enough household ammonia to make a paste and apply to the clay stains with a white cotton cloth. Let set for about 10 minutes and then launder in the hottest water safe for the fabric. You may have to repeat the process.

CLOTH DIAPERS: Scrape off any residue. Rinse diapers in cool water so stains don't set. Wash in hot, soapy water. Add a little bleach every 2 or 3 washes to remove stubborn stains, but run diapers through a second and final rinse, adding ½ cup vinegar to remove any bleach or soap residue. Note: Do not use fabric softener in every wash because it will cause the diapers to be less absorbent.

COFFEE/TEA: Rinse in cold water ASAP, and then rub in several drops of mild, white dishwashing liquid. Rinse well and then treat with a solution of 1 part white household vinegar and 3 parts water. Rinse again then launder as usual. Note: If you have used cream in your coffee, you may need to sponge the stain with dry-cleaning fluid.

COLA: Stains on 100 percent cotton, cotton blends, and permanent-press fabrics can be removed, if sponged with un-diluted white vinegar within 24 hours. Then launder or dry-clean according to manufacturer's directions.

COLLAR AND CUFF: To get out body oil stains, pretreat by rubbing liquid laundry detergent, hair shampoo or a prewash stain remover into the stain. Launder as usual.

CORDUROY: Check the care label to make sure these are machine washable. Turn garments inside-out and wash in warm or hot water. Hang and line dry; brush up nap.

CORRECTION FLUID: Because most correction fluids are latex-based, this kind of stain usually needs professional care. Let your dry cleaner know exactly what and where it is.

COUGH SYRUP/TUMMY MEDICATIONS: Scrape off any sticky stuff. Soak garment for 15 minutes in a mixture of water, liquid detergent and several drops of white vinegar. Then launder with appropriate bleach for the fabric. Sponge the affected area with dry-cleaning fluid.

CRAYON I: Scrape off excess wax with a dull knife or spoon. Place several layers of paper towel under the stained area and dab with dry-cleaning fluid until the crayon color is gone and no longer bleeding through to the towels. Using plenty of detergent, wash in the hottest water appropriate for the fabric.

CRAYON II: *If fabric has gone through the washer,* rub the stains with liquid laundry detergent then wash the garment with cold water and detergent. After the wash cycle, stop the washing machine and let the garment soak overnight. Next day, complete the wash cycle.

Clothing

CRAYON III: *If fabric has gone through the dryer*, spray both sides of the new stain with a petroleum-based, prewash stain remover and rub into the fabric. Let sit for a while and then wash as usual. If stains remain on a bleach-safe fabric, follow directions. (If there is crayon wax on the dryer drum, dampen a small cloth with the spray and then wipe out the drum. Be sure to then clean with a damp cloth.)

CRAYON IV: *If a crayon has gone through a whole load of clothes*, wash everything again with hot water, laundry soap, and 1 cup baking soda. If any color still remains, wash bleach-safe clothes with chlorine bleach or oxygen bleach in the hottest water that's safe for the fabric. Then launder as usual.

CREAM: Soak clothes in COLD water ASAP, and then rub liquid laundry detergent into the stain or treat with an enzyme presoak or prewash spray. Launder in the hottest water safe for the fabric. If the stain persists, sponge it with dry-cleaning fluid and launder a second time before putting into the dryer.

CURTAINS: To whiten sheers, use a whitener and brightener powder that's made for the washing machine. It's available in grocery or sewing stores in the section with fabric dyes. Follow directions exactly.

DEODORANT: See ANTIPERSPIRANT/DEODORANT

DOWN (comforters, jackets and vests): First read the care label instructions. If the garment can be machine washed, use a mild detergent on a gentle setting. Then put into the dryer on a low heat setting with a clean tennis ball to help redistribute down as it fluffs. You may want to take the item out and fluff by hand periodically during the drying process. If these garments have a musty smell, put them in the sun for a while. Some colored garments might need to be in the shade.

DYE TRANSFER: Use a packaged color remover to try to eliminate color from other fabrics that may have been transferred to white fabric. Follow label directions. Then launder. If dye remains on non-colorfast fabrics, soak in oxygen bleach then launder.

EASTER EGG DYE: Soak stain for at least 30 minutes in a prewash stain remover. Then launder as normal.

EGG: Using a dull-edged knife, scrape off as much residue as possible. Wet the area with cool water; pour on full-strength liquid laundry detergent and scrub the stain with a toothbrush. When the stain is gone, wash in the hottest water safe for the fabric.

EVENING CLOTHES (gowns, prom dresses): Fancy clothing that is heavily beaded or sequined may not be able to be washed or cleaned at home. Read the care instructions. Some garments can be spot-cleaned but others, like taffeta, cannot. Take these to a dry cleaner for consultation. But be aware that some beads (plastic) will dissolve when they come in contact with some dry-cleaning solutions or spot removers.

FABRIC-SOFTENER SHEETS: If fabrics are stained by contact with a fabric-softener (dryer) sheet, dampen stained area and rub with white bar soap. Rinse and launder as usual. Or, use liquid laundry detergent directly on the area, let set then wash in hot water. Check before drying to make sure the stain is gone.

FECES/STOOL: Remove solid residue from the fabric. Soak the garment in warm water and an enzyme detergent. After all traces of the stain are removed, launder as usual.

CAUTION: Always wear gloves when cleaning fecal matter.

FLOOD-STAINED FABRICS: If clothes have been soaked in muddy flood water, first get rid of as much dirt and residue as you can by shaking or brushing ASAP. Prewash fabrics in cool water with powdered laundry detergent. (Do not use hot water because it may set stains.) If garments have sewage, blood or grass stains, add an enzyme presoak to the prewash. For garments affected by motor oils or other heavy soils, use a prewash soil-and-stain remover. Use powdered detergent, which is more effective in getting rid of ground-in dirt and clay. Allow detergent to dissolve before adding clothes to the washer. Wash in small loads with a full water level. Use the hottest water safe for fabrics. Note: If clothing has been contaminated with sewage, be sure to add a disinfectant to the wash, such as liquid household bleach, if it's safe for the fabrics. There are many commercial products, which also can sanitize and control odors. Check the care labels. You may have to wash many times to get clean. Check the rinse water: If it's dirty, wash again; if it's clean the clothes should be clean. CAUTION: If there's iron in the soil deposits or water, bleach will make rust stains appear on fabrics. Don't put clothes into the dryer until the stains are gone. Heat will set them.

FRUIT/FRUIT JUICE/BERRIES: Get to them as fast as you can. Try one of these methods:

- Soak the stained area in cold water for about 30 minutes. Rub liquid laundry detergent into the wet area if there are remaining stains. Launder with detergent and warm water. If there are still stains, apply hydrogen peroxide to bleach-safe fabric, then rinse well.

- For washable fabric, soak in cold water. If stains are still there, dab white vinegar on them and rinse. If they are stubborn, apply hydrogen peroxide to bleach-safe fabrics.

- For "dry clean only" fabrics (read the care label), sponge with dry-cleaning fluid.

- Soak in cool water; wash. If stain remains, cover area with a paste made from oxygen-type bleach, several drops of hot water and a few drops of ammonia. Wait 15 to 30 minutes; then wash as usual.

FRUIT STAINS: To remove stains from hands, pour lemon juice on your hands and rub well. Rinse with water and dry.

GLOVES:

- *Gardening:* Shake off clay or dirt but leave gloves on to wash with soap and water. Remove and hang to dry.

- *White cotton:* Wash in a mild detergent then hold them under the faucet and run hot water into them just for several seconds. Rinse, let all water run out and dry flat.

Clothing

- *Winter gloves and mittens:* To dry, slip them over the tops of clean empty soda bottles. Read care label for cleaning instructions.

GLUE: To get quick-drying glue out of fabrics, first, attempt this home remedy: Wet a clean cloth with hot soapy water and put it on top of and underneath the spot where the glue spilled. Repeat every 15 minutes. Keep cloth hot (put into microwave for 10 to 15 seconds to heat). The hot cloth should soften the glue, which then can be peeled off the fabric. If this does not work, commercial solvents found at hardware stores will.

CAUTION: Read the directions before you use a commercial solvent and test on a small inconspicuous area to make certain it will not hurt the clothing.

GRASS, FLOWER and FOLIAGE: Use the following methods:

- *For washable fabrics:* Treat stains with prewash spray or apply liquid detergent into them. Using an enzyme detergent, wash in the hottest water designated for the fabric. Or, apply rubbing alcohol to the stained areas before laundering as usual.

- *For dry-cleanable only fabrics:* It may be safe to apply alcohol or sponge with dry-cleaning fluid but be sure to test on an inconspicuous spot first.

- *For acetate fabrics:* Sponge stains with nonflammable dry-cleaning solvent.

GRAVY: Use a spoon to scrape off all of it that you can. Blot the stain with white paper towels; then sprinkle cornstarch, salt, talcum powder, flour or artificial sweetener over the area and let set to absorb the grease. Brush off. Then treat with a laundry detergent and wash in the hottest water allowed for the fabric.

GREASE (motor oil, salad dressings, cooking oils): Try one or more of these methods:

- *To absorb oil,* rub in cornmeal, cornstarch or talcum powder and let set. Brush powder away. If fabric is washable, launder as above.

- *For washable fabrics,* pretreat with a heavy-duty liquid laundry detergent or a prewash spray. Then launder as usual.

- *For heavy stains on washable fabrics,* put stained areas facedown on paper towels. Apply dry-cleaning solvent to the backside of the stain; replace towels frequently. Let dry then rub in liquid detergent. Rinse and launder.

(See also SUEDE.)

HAIR DYE: These stains on fabric can be tough, if not impossible, to remove. Read the care label first and then dab area with appropriate bleach. Launder as normal. Do NOT use on silk or wool; instead apply a dab of hydrogen peroxide to the stain and watch to see if it starts to fade. CAUTION: Test on a hidden area first. Launder as usual.

ICE CREAM: Soak in cold water and then hand wash in warm soapy water. Rinse. If the ice cream was chocolate, or a greasy

Clothing

stain remains, sponge it with cleaning fluid. After all the stain is gone, launder as usual.

INK (ballpoint, felt-tip, liquid): Some of these stains may be impossible to remove, but first give pretreating a try with these methods:

- For dried stains, gently rub with isopropyl alcohol until the stain comes out. CAUTION: Do not apply to highly colored material.

- For spot removing, sponge the area around the stain with commercial dry-cleaning fluid. Then put the stain facedown on several layers of clean paper towels and apply cleaning fluid to the back of the stain. Rinse completely with water; launder as usual.

IODINE: Rinse with cool water from the backside of the stain. Soak in a solution of color remover, rinse and launder as usual.

JEANS: Acid-washed or other distressed jeans (with bleach) may yellow because chemicals used to create the look may not have been completely rinsed out or were exposed to strong heat or light. The yellow will not come out. Take them back to the store where you bought them or to the manufacturer for a refund or replacement.

LEATHER: Read care labels. Use special soaps, such as saddle soap that can be applied and removed with a moist cloth. For serious cleaning, take to a specialty professional dry cleaner.

LEATHER BOOTS: To prevent winter salt or chemical stains, along with water and snow, treat boots with a commercial protect-all or water-and stain-repellent spray *before* you wear for the first time. If they get stained, use specially made products, available at shoe-repair shops or in supermarkets.

LINEN: To remove yellow spots that have set on washable linen, soak in a commercial whitener and brightener, found alongside dyes in the grocery store. Then wash as usual.

LINGERIE: To get rid of yellowing in washable cotton, nylon or silk, soak for 30 minutes in a solution of 2 to 3 ounces of 3 percent hydrogen peroxide for each gallon of lukewarm water. Rinse and launder following care label instructions. You may have to repeat this process.

LIPSTICK: ASAP put the stained area on several layers of absorbent towel and saturate the garment with rubbing alcohol. CAUTION: Test a hidden spot for colorfastness. Then dip a cloth into rubbing alcohol and dab the area. Or, use a prewash spray

Clothing

on both sides of the fabric and work it in with a small brush. Rinse and launder as usual.

MAKEUP/FOUNDATION: Because water-based or powdered types of makeup are nongreasy, they can usually be removed by dampening the stained area; rubbing with white bar soap; rinsing and laundering as normal. Treat oily makeup stains with a prewash spray or liquid laundry detergent. Then dampen the area; rub to work the stain out. Rinse and launder in the hottest water safe for the fabric.

MASCARA: To remove water-based mascara, moisten the area and rub with liquid laundry detergent or white bar soap. Rinse and wash as usual. To remove oil-based mascara, apply prewash spray to the back of the stain, allow to set for several minutes then machine wash. Repeat if necessary.

MAYONNAISE: Get to this ASAP. Check the care label and pretreat with a prewash stain remover. Wash as usual. Check to make sure stain is gone before putting into the dryer.

MEAT JUICE: Soak first in cold or warm water with an enzyme presoak. Then wash as usual. Or soak in cold water and sprinkle *unseasoned* meat tenderizer on the stain and let it sit. Repeat if necessary and then wash.

MILDEW: Take the garment outside. Brush the mildew stain with a stiff brush to remove mold spores.

- *For bleachable fabrics*, soak for 15 minutes in a solution of 1 tablespoon chlorine bleach and 1 quart water. Rinse and launder, adding ½ cup chlorine bleach to the wash cycle.

- *For nonbleachable fabrics*, flush the stain with a solution of ½ cup lemon juice and 1 tablespoon salt. Dry the garment in the sun to "bleach out" the mildew stain. After all traces of stain are removed, launder as usual.

CAUTION: Some new white fabrics may have an optical brightener infused in the material and consequently the sun will turn them yellow.

MILK: ASAP soak clothes in cold water and then rub liquid laundry detergent into the stain or treat with an enzyme presoak or prewash spray. Launder in the hottest water safe for the fabric. If the stain persists, sponge it with dry-cleaning fluid and launder a second time before putting into the dryer.

MUCUS: Remove the residue from the fabric. Soak the garment in warm water and an enzyme detergent. After all traces of the stain are removed, launder as usual.

MUD: Allow the stain to dry completely. Using a stiff brush, brush away the dirt. Rub some liquid laundry detergent or prewash spray into the remaining stain. Launder as usual. If the stain is heavy, pretreat with an enzyme detergent.

MUSTARD: First, dampen the area and then rub liquid laundry detergent into the stain. Rinse and then soak in hot water with detergent for several hours. Use an enzyme detergent for final laundering.

MYSTERY STAINS: Always check clothing for spots and stains before you store. Deal with spots and stains when you find them. If caught early, these stains may be soluble in water, so flush the stain ASAP with cold water. Put prewash spray on the stain and rub. Launder as normal after all traces of the stain are gone.

If stains are old and yellowish, they may have been created by spills from light-colored sugary drinks like apple juice, soda pop, and white wine or even from oils such as body lotion, mayonnaise, and salad dressing. If not noticed and the clothes are stored, the heat in a warm closet may have caused them to turn yellow or brown. They are difficult to remove.

For *washable fabrics,* try to lighten by using a heavy-duty detergent and all-fabric bleach for color or household chlorine bleach for bleachable whites.

For *oil-based stains* (you may notice jagged, irregular edges), set the temperature for the hottest water safe for the fabric. If you're uncertain, use warm water.

NAIL POLISH: Use one of these methods:

Sponge the stain with pure acetone *after testing a hidden area for colorfastness.* Launder as usual. Note: Do NOT use acetone on fabrics containing acetate or triacetate because it will dissolve them. For acetate fabrics, use amyl acetate, which is safe.

Or: Put the stain facedown on several layers of paper towel. Sponge the backside with nail polish remover, which is fragrance- and color-free and contains no additives. Replace the towels, as needed, and repeat until stain is gone. Launder as usual. Note: Do not use nail polish remover on acetate; it will do damage. Instead, send to dry cleaner.

NEEDLEPOINT: Cleaning will depend on type of thread (wool or synthetic) and canvas used. Some colors are not safe to wash. First, try to lift off dust and dirt with a vacuum. Use the brush attachment and hold ½ inch above needlepoint; do not touch the thread because it may be fragile. If there are other stains, check with your local arts and crafts store or dry cleaner before you do anything else.

OIL/GREASE/BUTTER/MARGARINE: Greasy or oily stains need pretreatment with a prewash spray. Then rub liquid laundry detergent into the dampened stain. When the stain is gone, launder with plenty of detergent in the hottest water safe for the fabric.

ORANGE-COLORED STAINS: French salad dressing or spaghetti sauce can leave orange stains on garments. Dampen a cotton napkin with water then moisten with a squeeze of lemon juice or small amount of white vinegar. Blot the stain until it disappears. Rinse in clear water. Use this method on synthetic fiber, cottons and drip-dry clothes, but do NOT use on silk.

PAINT: Don't let the paint dry on fabrics if possible. Scrape off any fresh paint, and then get to stains immediately. Treatment differs based on type of paint but always check the care label first:

Clothing

- *Oil-based or varnish:* If the fabric is color-safe, use a bit of turpentine or paint thinner, then rinse well in water. Rub with a paste of powdered detergent and water; wash as usual. Or, sponge with nonflammable dry-cleaning solvent. Launder.

- *Paint thinned with solvents:* Dab some of the solvent onto the stained area. After the area is wet with solvent, work a bit of liquid laundry detergent into it and soak in hot water. Launder as usual.

- *Water-based:* Often will wash out with just soap and water. But if the paint has set and dried, it will be more difficult to remove. Rinse stain in warm water to flush out paint; launder as usual.

PENCIL LEAD: Use a clean pencil eraser to gently erase as much of the lead stain as you can. Rub liquid laundry detergent into the remaining stain and then launder as usual.

PERFUME: Use cool water to soak or sponge the stain immediately. Then pour a bit of white household vinegar on a sponge and apply to the stain. Rinse. If any stain remains, rub liquid laundry detergent into it and launder as usual.

PERSPIRATION: Rub area with bar soap; then launder in hottest water safe for fabric. If stains remain, wash again with enzyme detergents or oxygen bleach in hottest water safe for fabric. Note: If a perspiration stain has affected the color of the fabric, sponge a bit of white vinegar on the stain. Then rinse and launder again.

PLASTIC ("rubber" baby pants): Use the delicate cycle and wash on warm. Always protect small items by putting into a mesh bag. Dry on warm and take out after 5 to 10 minutes.

PLAY PUTTY: Rub liquid laundry detergent into the spot and then scrub it from the underside of the fabric. Treat stain with diluted hydrogen peroxide (test in an inconspicuous area first) and then wash in the hottest water safe for the fabric.

RING AROUND THE COLLAR: Rub liquid laundry detergent or prewash spray or hair shampoo into the area and let this work on the stain for 30 minutes. Or, rub area with white bar soap on a damp sponge and launder in the hottest water safe for the fabric.

RUBBER CEMENT: Use an ice cube or ice pack to harden the cement. Or: Put garment in the freezer, and then scrape off with a dull knife. Saturate the area with a prewash stain remover. Rinse and launder as usual.

RUST: Commercial rust removers found in the fabric dye section of your grocery store will do the job. Follow the label directions exactly. Never use the rust remover near or inside a washer because it can remove the glossy finish on the porcelain outside or inside the machine.

Alternatively, you can give white vinegar a try, but NEVER use bleach on rust stains. For a small rust stain, sprinkle it with salt and rub with half a lemon. Set out in the sun to help "bleach" it out. Note: Some white fabrics should not be put into the sun. Read care label.

Clothing

RUSTY DISCOLORATION ON WHITE FABRIC: Use phosphate detergent (if available) in wash, along with 1 cup enzyme detergent or oxygen bleach. If stains persist, dissolve 1 ounce oxalic acid crystals per gallon of water in a plastic container. Soak clothes for 10 to 15 minutes. Rinse and launder.

SALAD DRESSING: Remove as much of the liquid as you can. Sponge area with cleaning fluid to get rid of the grease; then treat remaining stain with a prewash product. Launder as usual with appropriate bleach, if needed. Read care label and test on hidden area of fabric first.

SAP: It may be possible to remove tree sap from washable garments by using a stain remover that contains dry-cleaning solvent, but read the directions first and test an area for colorfastness. Then put the stained area facedown on several layers of paper towel and apply the solvent from the back.

Alternatively, make a paste of powder or liquid laundry detergent (without bleach) and ammonia. Apply to the spot and let it sit for 30 minutes, then launder. Repeat paste step if needed.

SCORCH MARKS: Heavily scorched fabric cannot be returned to its original state. Try one of these removal methods but always read care labels first:

- For *bleachable* fabrics: Launder with chlorine bleach.

- For *nonbleachable* fabrics: Soak in enzyme detergent or oxygen bleach and the hottest water safe for fabric and then launder.

- For *colorfast* fabrics: Always test a hidden area for color-fastness first then use a clean white cloth to dab 3 percent hydrogen peroxide on the scorched area to fade light scorch marks on fabrics. You may have to apply several times, but scorch marks will lessen.

- For *delicate* fabrics: Rub scorch marks lightly with a clean white cloth dampened with white vinegar. Wipe with a clean, dry cloth.

SEMEN: Pretreat with a laundry product containing enzymes. Launder with oxygen bleach.

SHOE DYE/POLISH: To remove shoe dye or polish from off-white hose, soak the discolored section of the hose in rubbing alcohol and wash as usual. If you need to use a color-remover, treat the entire hose because it may change the overall appearance. Note: To keep dye from bleeding on hose, spray the inside of shoes several times with a fabric-protector spray and repeat occasionally.

SHOE POLISH: Some shoe polish, especially liquid, may not come out. But try these methods:

- For *liquid shoe polish*, pretreat with a paste of powder or liquid detergent and water. Then launder as normal. Or, apply cleaning fluid to the stain; then wash the garment in detergent and warm water.

Clothing

- For *paste shoe polish*, use a dull knife and scrape residue off. Pretreat with a prewash stain remover and rinse well. Launder using a color-safe bleach.

SILK FABRIC: CAUTION: Silk: First, read the care label to see if the item can be hand- or machine-washed. Use warm to cool water and wash gently. Lengthy soaking can damage colors; chlorine bleach and excessive rubbing will damage delicate silk fiber. Iron on low or steam settings.

Never try to remove spill stains on silk by rubbing the area because silk fibers break easily. Blot instead.

- *Beverage spills:* These may disappear when the fabric dries, but sugar in some drinks may create a yellow stain that appears later. Take silk garments to the dry cleaner as soon as possible. Let the counter person know exactly what was spilled where.

- *Perspiration/body oils:* These are silk's worst enemies. Maintain silk garments with regular dry cleaning or handwashing.

SOUR CREAM: ASAP soak clothes in cold water and then rub liquid laundry detergent into the stain or treat with an enzyme presoak or prewash spray. Launder in the hottest water safe for the fabric. If the stain persists, sponge it with cleaning fluid and launder a second time before putting the clothes into the dryer.

STICKY RESIDUE: This gluey stuff left behind from gummed stickers can be removed by carefully dabbing the area with a petroleum-based prewash spray or cleaning fluid, depending on the care label.

SUEDE I: Surface dirt stains can be removed by gently rubbing the material with an art gum eraser or lightly buffing the spots with the fine side of an emery board. Or: Pat cornstarch or flour into a minor oil-type stain to soak it up, brush off, then, wipe the surface with a damp, clean cloth. Let it dry and then brush with a clothes brush to bring up the nap. Stubborn or difficult stains should be removed by a professional dry cleaner that deals with suede and leather.

SUEDE II: To treat grease or other heavy stains effectively, the only solution is to take the garment to a specialty professional dry cleaner.

For an *emergency treatment*, pat talcum powder or cornstarch onto the fabric to absorb grease. Brush off excess then sponge out the grease with a cloth dipped in white vinegar. Use a suede brush to restore the nap. CAUTION: Test vinegar on a hidden spot before sponging it on the fabric.

Maintain suede with regular brushing using a special suede brush. If it gets dusty, wipe with a damp cloth. Do not store suede in plastic bags because it needs air circulation.

SUEDE (imitation): Launder in a washing machine set on delicate cycle, cold water, and use a mild detergent. Line dry.

SUNSCREEN/SUNTAN LOTIONS: Some contain oil to make them moisture-resistant and this oil is not easy to remove. Read the manufacturer's directions before applying. Make sure the products are dry before you put on your clothes and wash your hands after you have applied lotions before you touch clothing. If you do get any on a garment, check the care label and pretreat the stain ASAP. Launder as usual. Or: To lift greasy sunscreens, sprinkle a bit of cornstarch on the stains and let sit for several minutes. Brush off gently and then launder as usual.

For a stain on the neckline of white clothes, treat with a solvent (spot remover) or prewash spray because many sunscreens contain oil. Wash as usual using the warmest water safe for the fabric. Don't put into the dryer unless you are certain that all of the stain is gone. Repeat the process if necessary. If the stain has not been removed, take the garment to a dry cleaner.

SWEATERS: Read the care label first in determining how to remove a stain; it will depend on fiber type. Some can be hand-washed and then blocked-dried; others can be machine washed on the gentle cycle. Be sure to use the laundry detergent indicated for the fiber. If the label says dry clean only, take to a cleaner or use an in-dryer kit, which can remove light soil and odors.

Check for colorfastness on a hidden spot before you use stain removal methods.

SWIMSUIT: To prevent fading/fabric damage from pool-water chlorine, buy chorine remover for aquarium water, which is available at pet stores. Soak your bathing suit after each swim in a solution of 1 drop anti-chlorine formula in 1 gallon water. Don't rinse out.

TAR: For washable fabrics, first remove any residue of tar. Wash with detergent as usual. Or, use a cleaning fluid; place stain facedown on paper towels to absorb the tar. Launder in hottest water safe for fabric.

TEA: On washable fabric, rinse area and soak with cold water. Then use a prewash spray to treat the stain. Wash as usual. Because tea contains tannin, the stain may come back. Treat again and wash as usual. Nonwashables will need to be professionally dry cleaned.

TENNIS SHOES: To remove stains from white rubber shoes, use a whitewall tire cleaner. Follow directions on the label.

TIES: To prevent serious stains, before you wear a tie the first time, spray it with a fabric stain-repellent. To treat stains on silk ties see SILK FABRIC. Read the care label for cleaning instructions. Dry cleaning may be the only answer.

TOBACCO: Dampen stain and rub with bar soap. Rinse. Then soak in enzyme detergent or oxygen bleach. Launder. If stain still remains, launder again with chlorine bleach, if it's safe for the fabric. Check care label.

TOMATO KETCHUP/BARBECUE SAUCE: Scrape off any stain excess and then soak the garment in cold water for a half hour. While the item is still wet, rub white bar soap or liquid laundry detergent into any remaining stains. Launder in warm water and detergent.

On 100 percent cotton, cotton blends, or permanent press, within 24 hours sponge undiluted white vinegar to remove stain. Then launder or dry-clean as the manufacturer recommends.

TOOTHPASTE ON FABRIC: CAUTION: Do not use this treatment on silk or delicate fabrics as the rubbing motion could break the fibers. Put a cloth underneath the fabric and work with a damp cloth to remove the toothpaste; then blow-dry garment with a hair dryer.

An Ounce of Prevention

To avoid toothpaste stains on your clothes, wear a small towel "bib" under your chin while brushing. Or, better yet, brush your teeth before putting on clothes!

T-SHIRT/WASHABLE SHIRT: To remove underarm stains, before laundering, sponge the stained area with white household vinegar and allow to sit for a couple of minutes. If you still see stains, apply a paste of water and an enzyme laundry detergent or an enzyme presoak. Let soak for several hours and then wash garment in the hottest water safe for the shirt's fabric.

URINE: Soak the stained area in warm water. If any stain remains, sponge the area with a solution of half white household vinegar and half water. (This also helps to neutralize any leftover odor.) Rinse well and launder as usual.

URINE RESIDUE: Flush the stain as soon as possible and then soak in warm water with an enzyme detergent. For bleachable fabric, launder as usual and add chlorine bleach to the wash load. For other fabrics, add an all-fabric bleach to the wash load to help eliminate any remaining stain.

VELVET: To eliminate water stains on velvet, hold the wet area over steam spouting from a teakettle for just a few minutes. Shake garment and let dry. Brush up nap.

VELVETEEN: See CORDUROY.

VOMIT: Get rid of any solid residue from the fabric. Soak the garment in warm water and an enzyme detergent; you can add baking soda to the rinse too. After all traces of the stain are removed, launder as usual.

WEDDING DRESS: When you buy a wedding dress, ask about the cleaning care and get written care instructions. Read the care label BEFORE you buy. The fabric and trims may be difficult to clean. You will want to preserve this special-day garment and pay attention to how you can do that when you purchase. For example, because wedding dresses of-

> ### Dryer Hints
>
> *Did you know that dust and lint buildup in dryers is a leading cause of home fires? So, for safety's sake, clean the lint filter after each load and the exhaust duct of your dryer on a regular basis.*
>
> *If you leave clothes in the dryer too long, put a big damp towel in the dryer with the wrinkled clothes. Set the dryer for 15 minutes and when it's done, take it out right away. Presto, wrinkles are gone!*

ten have trims of beads, embroidery, seed pearls, appliqué, or sequins that have been glued on, the adhesives are soluble and might dissolve in dry-cleaning solvent.

Polystyrene buttons, beads and imitation pearl beads also may dissolve in the solvent. Some imitation pearl beads are polystyrene with a hard shell covering. Polystyrene will dissolve in

Clothing

perchloroethylene, which is the most common dry-cleaning solvent. So the beads will disappear and leave just the enamel shell. However, if the pearl bead is glued on rather than sewn on, often the glue or adhesive is not resistant to solvent.

Sequins that are held on with adhesives rather than being sewn on are not resistant to solvent either. In some cases sequins can shrivel or curl if exposed to heat or moisture used in cleaning. Glitter is very fragile, and if it's been glued on, it may come off during cleaning. Metal or glitter trim can also corrode, oxidize or change color.

Silk, taffeta, brocade, chiffon, and organza fabrics require special care. As soon after the wedding as possible, take the dress to be dry-cleaned by a professional—even if it looks clean! It may have spots from perspiration, body oils, perfume or hairspray, which you can't see. There also could be food or beverage stains that will oxidize and set in later. Be sure to tell the dry cleaner about any cleaning method you already have tried. Point out any stains and let the dry cleaner examine the gown carefully. Also have them make any repairs of small tears.

If you are wearing an heirloom or antique gown, follow these hints: Take the dress to a dry cleaner who specializes in restoring antique fabrics. Tell the dry cleaner how old the dress is and what the fabric is. Show the cleaner the stained areas and point out any weak fabric or loose trim.

WHITE FABRICS TURNED GRAY: Dissolve 1 tablespoon borax in a cup of hot water and add to the final rinse to help whites become white again. An old-fashioned bluing agent that you add to laundry or a whitener and brightener may work, too.

WHITE NYLON, POLYESTER (durable press turned yellow): Soak garment overnight with enzyme detergent or oxygen bleach. Then launder in the hottest water safe for fabric with detergent and bleach-safe for these fabrics. Or: Launder with enzyme detergent or oxygen bleach added to regular detergent and in the hottest water safe for fabric. Do not dry these modern fabrics in the sun because they may contain fluorescent brighteners, which react badly to the sun.

WHITE SILK (turned yellow): If the garment is washable, soak it in a plastic container or sink for 2 or 3 hours in a mixture of 1 gallon warm water with 2 ounces of 3 percent hydrogen peroxide. Remove, rinse in warm water. Dry on a plastic hanger.

WINE: Soak stained area in cool water. If the material is bleach-safe, use bleach (follow washing instructions) or electric dishwasher detergent (make a paste with a bit of water) and scrub with an old, clean toothbrush. After spot treating, wash in the hottest water possible for the fabric. For 100 percent cotton, cotton blends, and permanent press, sponge stain with undiluted white vinegar within 24 hours; then launder or dry-clean according to the manufacturer's instructions.

WOOLENS:

- *For hand washables*, wash in cool water with a mild soap or bleach-free detergent. Soak for 3 to 5 minutes. Rinse several times in clean water. Gently squeeze—don't ring—out excess water. Lay out flat to dry and do not put in sunlight or in direct heat.

Clothing

- *For machine washables,* use a mild, bleach-free detergent on the warm, gentle cycle. Add detergent to the machine as it fills to dissolve before putting garment in. Hang to dry.

PART FOUR

Carpets, Rugs, and Floors

H ere at Heloise central, we get more questions about carpet stains than just about anything else. I guess that's because there are millions of acres of carpet just waiting for the next accident to happen. The following hints will come to the rescue to help remove carpet stains, heel marks from the kitchen floor, oily blotches in the garage floor and dozens of other unwanted marks and spots!

Caring for Carpets

Curiously, some carpet stains result from how you may clean your carpet. Consider these questions the next time you're ready to treat your carpet to a general cleaning:

- What cleaning product will loosen or dissolve dirt or the stain without damaging the carpet?

- Has the cleaning agent been left on the carpet long enough to do the job?

- How has the dirt been removed and where has it been taken?

If you've noticed that carpets just seem to get dirty very soon after being cleaned, that may indicate that the dirt was not really removed, but rather washed back down into the pile of the carpet. It reappears when the carpet gets used. If the carpet shampoo is not removed properly from carpet fibers, it actually attracts dirt!

Because there are so many possible problems with carpet cleaning, it just may be better to use a professional service for overall cleaning and big stains. Think about it: Your carpet is an expensive household item to replace if you make any mistakes.

4 Basic Commercial Carpet Cleaning Methods

1. Hot-water extraction. Cleaning solution is sprayed directly onto the carpet and then a vacuum pump (usually mounted on a vehicle) extracts (sucks up) the dirt and soil. This method is popular but has limitations because it does not agitate the pile, so it may not pick up deep dirt in the pile. Also, the cleaning liquid has only a limited

time to work because it is immediately vacuumed up again.

2. Rotary shampooing. A floor machine with a powerful electric motor and circular brush loosens the pile of the carpet. Shampoo is released through openings in the brush, and as it spins, the shampoo is whipped into a foam. It lifts out and suspends the dirt. When the foam dries into powdery flakes, it can be vacuumed up.

3. Dry-cleaning compound. Dry-cleaning solvents and detergents are applied to the carpet and brushed in. This loosens soil, and after drying, the dirt is suspended and vacuumed up with an upright vacuum. Best of all, any compound left behind continues to clean until it is removed by subsequent vacuuming. This method is good for homeowners because water is not involved and over-wetting does not become a problem. This method is most effective.

4. Foam cleaning. Foam spray cleaners can be purchased at a supermarket and used with a sponge or brush. Remove the foam with a vacuum or thick towel. Done by professionals with mechanical units, which generate foam from a liquid concentrate, the foam is worked into the carpet with cylindrical brushes and removed by a vacuum. This method is good for regular maintenance rather than heavy-duty cleaning because it does not get into the pile as thoroughly as rotary shampooing.

Heloise's Favorite Home Cleaners for Carpet Stains

Ammonia solution: Mix ½ cup water with 1 tablespoon clear household ammonia, which translates to 8 parts water to 1 part ammonia for larger quantities. CAUTION: If ammonia is used improperly, if could cause a color change. Always test in a hidden area first.

Baking soda: In a paste form, baking soda neutralizes acids. In powdered form, it helps to absorb odors.

Dry-cleaning solvents: Use a small amount of this commercial spotter or volatile dry spotter because too much can harm carpet backings. Use a cloth or sponge to apply to spot or stain; never pour directly onto carpet. CAUTION: Do NOT use lighter fluid, carbon tetrachloride or gasoline.

Hydrogen peroxide, 3 percent: Use this percentage or sodium perborate. CAUTION: Do NOT use chlorine bleach on any carpeting.

Liquid detergent solution: Choose a neutral dish detergent diluted with water in parts of about 20 to 1. CAUTION: Do NOT use automatic dishwasher detergent because it may contain bleaching solutions, which could damage carpet fibers. NEVER use a laundry detergent of any kind because it may contain optical brighteners (fluorescent dyes), which may affect the colors.

Non-oily nail polish remover (acetone or amyl acetate): There are 2 types of nail polish removers: One with acetone, which is a dry-cleaning solvent (apply as indicated above). The other contains amyl acetate. CAUTION: Do NOT use amyl acetate on carpets because it may melt some fibers. Read the carpet labels or manufacturer's material for fiber content.

White vinegar: Dilute 50–50 with water for rinsing. Also, keep these household items on hand for easy cleanups:

Denatured alcohol
Hairspray
Paint thinner
Prewash spray
Commercial rust remover

Preventing Stains Is Easier Than Cleaning Them Up!

There really are ways to avoid stains and prevention lessens the stress of dealing with these minor household emergencies. Be prepared by having home cleaning supplies—and my hints at hand!

- Buy soil-retardant, antistatic carpets or have your existing ones treated with soil retardant. Place large mats at all entrances to your home to stop dirt from being tracked into the house.

- Put plastic sheets on the floor under chairs or highchairs where children will be eating because they WILL spill food and drink.

Carpets, Rugs, and Floors

Heloise's Top 7 Carpet Spot-and-Stain Removal Tips

1. ASAP: Work on stains as soon as possible before they have a chance to soak in or set.

2. Pretest: Before beginning to clean a spot, pretest cleaner in a hidden spot (under a piece of furniture or in a corner of a closet). If the color changes or color comes off on the cloth, it's probably time to call in a professional, or change cleaners.

3. Gently does it: Use only small amounts of cleaning agents; blot gently and frequently. Never brush or rub vigorously. However, with many fabrics, if you rub gently going in both directions it causes a small static-electric charge known as an ionic transfer, which helps to loosen the dirt at a molecular level. Blotting alone does not create the electric charge needed to clean the soil.

4. Outside in: To prevent rings or spreading of the stain, always work from the outer edge of the spot toward the center. After all stains have been cleaned, gently rinse the spot with water and absorb all moisture with a clean towel or white paper towels.

5. Cleaner of choice: White vinegar is one of the best cleaners for removing spots and stains on carpeting. Using the right cloth is important in cleanup, too.

6. The best cloth for the job: Cloth made of linen, the most absorbent material, or a blend of 80 percent linen and 20 percent cotton do the best job. Microfiber cloth works well, too.

7. Throwing in the towel: Sometimes only a professional cleaner can help!

- Store all hazardous chemicals—insecticides, oven cleaners, plant food, toilet cleaners—in one safe place, in a garage cupboard and in safe containers, too. Remove only to use and then put back immediately to minimize spots and spills, which could cause damage of one kind or another. Or, explore the possibility of using environmentally friendly alternatives, which are less likely to stain or bleach if spilled.

- Get rid of heavy-duty stain makers, unless you have to have them. Permanent markers or non-washable paints should not be stored in the house if you have children. Guide your children to enjoying drinks that aren't red! Reds are the worst stains.

- Choose modern antiseptic ointments, which are clear and nonstaining, over iodine and other older antiseptics, which do stain.

- Some acne medications can cause serious stains or can actually bleach fabrics and paint on walls. Wash hands after applying these medications to avoid staining.

  If you have teenagers who use these creams, think about keeping a roll of paper towels in the bathroom for them to use. This will save your pretty towels.

Carpet Stains A-to-Z

ACID CHEMICALS: Strong chemicals, such as oven or drain cleaners, most likely will create permanent bleaching of carpet color. Sponge stained area with water to dilute acid and to help to wash it away. Then sponge area with a solution of 1 tablespoon baking soda to 1 quart of warm water. If the stain persists, apply an ammonia solution (1 part ammonia to 8 parts water), test in a hidden spot, rinse with cold water and blot.

ACNE MEDICATIONS: These contain benzoyl peroxide, which can destroy carpet dyes. It may take months before the chemical is activated by humidity or moisture. The affected area will then be bleached white with an orange or pink halo on the outer edges—now you know what that mystery stain is! To find out if this medication is the culprit, test it on a scrap piece of the same carpet and moisten it with tap water. Place in a microwave for 10 to 15 seconds. It should discolor just as the affected area of the carpet has done. Unfortunately, this stain cannot be removed. Either rearrange your furniture to cover it or patch it (See HOW TO PATCH CARPET, page 108).

ALCOHOLIC BEVERAGES/PERFUME: Blot up the spill right away, then apply a detergent solution and blot again. Follow with diluted white vinegar and blot. Then apply ammonia solution and blot. If a red-wine stain remains, try using a little 3 to 5 percent hydrogen peroxide and let set for 24 hours to check color. Test on an inconspicuous area first. Finally, rinse with water and blot until dry.

ASPHALT/TAR: Scrape off as much as you can with a dull knife or spatula. Test a hidden area with dry-cleaning solvent, then apply the solvent or paint thinner. Blot, working from the outside to the center. Rinse with tap water and dry.

BABY FORMULA/CREAM/MILK/ICE CREAM: Wipe off excess first then apply ammonia solution or a detergent with enzymes because the enzymes will digest (eat) the protein. Be careful with carpets containing wool because the enzymes will eat the wool too if left on. Rinse completely with cool-to-warm water and blot dry.

BLEACH SPOTS: If you've accidentally spilled a bit of bleach on carpet, recolor small spots by mixing food coloring or clothing dye with water to make the right matching shade. Apply by dabbing with a cotton swab, and if it fades, just reapply. A permanent felt-tip marker might do the job in a pinch.

BLOOD: Apply cool detergent solution and blot. Follow with ammonia solution and blot again. Rinse with cool water and blot. If the stain persists, use an enzyme detergent (pretest on hidden area first). Rinse and blot again. If all else fails bleaching with 3 to 5 percent hydrogen peroxide may work.

BURN MARKS: Remove light burns by rubbing with an emery board or trim away damaged yarns with scissors. Carpet burns from cigarettes create holes. To repair them, trim the damaged yarns down to the backing. Use a toothpick to dab rubber cement into the hole. Put a bit of cement on the end of yarns taken from an unseen area of the carpet; insert into the hole. Let dry and trim to merge in. If the damage is too overwhelming, patch the area (See HOW TO PATCH CARPET pp. 108) or have a professional do it.

BUTTER/MARGARINE: Use a dull knife or a spoon to scrape off as much as possible. Apply dry-cleaning solvent and then blot

Carpets, Rugs, and Floors

How to Patch Carpet

A burn mark or permanent stain may make it necessary to patch your carpet. A professional can do the job, but, if you are the least bit handy, you can do it yourself! Here's how:

1. Remove all of the damaged area by cutting a square or rectangle with a sharp carpet cutter or utility knife. Cut clean and straight edges through the carpet and backing with one stroke. Take care not to damage the padding or the floor. (If possible you could slip a piece of heavy cardboard or wood under the affected area to protect the floor.)

2. Cut a patch from a remnant of the same carpet (or from a hidden space in a closet) in the exact same pattern, size, design and pile direction as the damaged area. If the carpet has a regular pattern, or no pattern at all, cut the patch by placing the damaged piece facedown on the back of the remnant. Use the stitching to line up the piece to be cut out. On irregularly patterned carpet, line up the pattern carefully from the top. Check for fit.

3. Spread a thin layer of carpet adhesive on the underside of the patch along its edges and along the edges of the surrounding carpet. Press the patch into place then redistribute the pile with your fingers to disguise the seams. Let the glue set for as long as possible before walking on the area.

with a detergent solution. Rinse with clear water and blot until dry.

CANDLE WAX: Freeze the dripped wax with an ice cube placed in a plastic bag to harden, then scrape off as much wax as possible with a dull knife. Put several white paper towels over the wax and press over it on a WARM setting. Repeat process using clean towels until all wax is removed. If any residue remains, use a bit of dry-cleaning solvent and blot.

CANDY: Scrape off solid sticky pieces with a dull knife. Apply ammonia solution and blot. Then use a detergent solution, rinse and blot dry.

CHEWING GUM: Fill a plastic bag with ice cubes and place it over the gum to harden. Then gently scrape off the sticky stuff with a dull table knife to remove as much of the gum as possible. Remove the rest of the stain with a dry-cleaning solvent (available at grocery or shoe stores). Be sure to follow the directions on the package exactly.

CHOCOLATE: Scrape off any excess and start working on the stain with a cool detergent solution. Follow with an ammonia solution and then a vinegar solution. Rinse and blot.

COFFEE: Dab with cool water. Add a drop of mild white dishwashing liquid to 1 cup water and apply to stain. Rinse. If stain remains, treat with a mixture of 1 part white household vinegar with 3 parts water. Rinse.

CRAYON: Apply dry-cleaning solvent; then use detergent solution and hot water. Rinse and blot dry.

DYES: Beverages, cosmetics, medicines and foods can contain dyes that stain when they are absorbed into the fibers. Try a detergent solution, rinse and blot dry until no color shows up

Carpets, Rugs, and Floors

on your cleaning cloth. Rinse with a solution of half water, half denatured alcohol with a splash of vinegar. If the stain does not come out, it's time to call a professional carpet cleaner.

EGG: Scrape off leftover bits. Wash with cool (not hot) water and detergent to remove grease. Rinse and blot dry.

FELT-TIP PEN: Begin with a detergent solution unless the pen is marked permanent then use dry-cleaning solvent first. If the stain persists, try ammonia solution. Rinse and blot dry.

FRINGE: The fringe on about 70 percent of new rugs is made of cotton; older Orientals have wool fringe. To clean, begin by combing out fringe carefully. To protect the floor, make a pad to put under the fringe by placing a towel over a plastic garbage bag. Use a solution of 1 tablespoon nonsudsing ammonia with 8 ounces warm water. Apply with a clean white cloth or sponge, dabbing the fringe. Rinse with a solution of 1 tablespoon white household vinegar and 8 ounces warm water. If the fringe still looks dirty, you may have to take the rug to a professional cleaner.

FRUIT/FRUIT JUICE/BERRIES: Fruit stains are among the most difficult to remove. Rinse completely with cool-to-warm water then blot. CAUTION: Do not use hot water because heat sets sugar. Apply a vinegar solution, blot. Rinse with water, blot dry. You may have to use a bleaching agent, if the carpet will tolerate it. Test in a hidden area first.

FURNITURE POLISH: Wipe up spilled polish ASAP. Begin working on the stain with a dry-cleaning fluid then wash with detergent solution, rinse and blot.

GRASS: Sponge stains with denatured alcohol. CAUTION: Test in a hidden spot first, because alcohol can make colors run. If the stain remains, apply ammonia solution. Rinse. Try a vinegar solution. Rinse and blot dry. If that stubborn stain still is there, give 3 to 5 percent hydrogen peroxide a try.

HAIR DYE: It's so difficult to remove this stain—particularly from carpet. The most important thing you can do is to act right away. First, blot up the hair dye with white paper towels. Then, mix ¼ teaspoon of a liquid dishwashing detergent with 1 cup of lukewarm water. Do NOT use a stronger concentration of this solution. CAUTION: Never use laundry detergents or automatic dishwashing detergents. They could damage the carpet further. Put a small amount of the mixture on a white cloth. Dab from the outside of the stain to the center to stop it from spreading. Let it stay on the spill for a minute or two then blot it again. Continue this as long as you see the hair dye on the cloth. You may have to repeat this process several times. Have patience. If the stain is gone, rinse the area with cold water. Then blot up the moisture with a dry cloth.

If you haven't gotten to it fast enough and spots remain, try this as a last resort: Lighten the spots first with 3 percent hydrogen peroxide. Using a cotton swab, dab a little and let dry for 24 hours before trying again. Then buy a felt-tip fabric marker that best matches the color of your carpet. Be light-handed in

Carpets, Rugs, and Floors

dabbing this on the spots. Do a little bit at a time. Leave overnight and see how it blends in.

INDIA INK: Unlike fountain-pen ink, which is water-soluble and comes out with a detergent solution, India ink can leave a permanent mark. Begin with a dry-cleaning solvent and follow with a detergent solution. Blot well. Then apply ammonia solution; rinse and blot dry.

INDOOR/OUTDOOR CARPETS: Prewash spray should get stains out of indoor/outdoor carpeting. Test it on a hidden area to make sure it won't discolor the carpet. Spray the stain. Let set for several minutes, then rinse well. If carpeting is outside, rinse off with a hose.

INK: CAUTION: Pretest a hidden area of the carpet no matter which solution you use to get rid of ink stains.

Lift off light ink stains with a cotton swab or clean cloth moistened with dry-cleaning solvent or isopropyl alcohol.

Remove heavier marks with dry-cleaning solvent and blot; then use denatured or isopropyl alcohol and blot. And finally, try nonoily nail polish remover (acetone).

INK-JET (See TONER CARTRIDGE)

INSECTICIDES: Unless the label indicates otherwise, insecticides should not be applied directly to carpets because they can be permanently damaged if the insecticide interacts with carpet colors, which could become discolored. If you have to use insecticides in your home in areas where there are carpets, spray on the baseboards.

IODINE: Begin working on it with denatured alcohol. Then rub with ammonia solution; blot, rinse and blot dry.

JAM/JELLY: Rinse thoroughly with cool water. Then apply a vinegar solution; blot, rinse again and blot dry.

MINERAL OIL: Get to it fast. If it's a small drop or two, pour a small amount of rubbing alcohol onto a paper towel and blot—do NOT rub—the oil from the outside of the stain toward the center. If it's a bigger spill, use a dry-cleaning solvent. Pour the solvent onto a paper towel, and blot from the outside of the stain to the center. You may have to repeat this process. Check the padding to make sure the oil has not leaked onto it. If it has, you may need to call a professional to clean it.

MUD: Let mud dry completely before brushing off. Treat stain with detergent solution, rinse and blot. If any stain remains, try dry-cleaning solvent. Repeat, repeat, repeat!

MUSTARD: Apply a vinegar solution then blot. If the stain persists, give rust remover (oxalic acid solution) a try. CAUTION: Do not use ammonia or alkali bleach.

NAIL POLISH: Carefully apply dry-cleaning solvent. If it doesn't work, use acetone (non-oily nail polish remover), but pretest a hidden area first. Do not pour it on!

Carpets, Rugs, and Floors

OVEN CLEANER/STRONG ALKALI: If you spill oven cleaner, which is usually lye (a strong alkali), act quickly to avoid damage, especially on wool blends. Blot up all you can with a cloth or paper towels, then rinse completely with vinegar solution to neutralize the alkali. Blot and repeat; then rinse, blot and dry.

PAINT: Blot and soak up any type of paint immediately, whatever kind of paint it is. Do not rub because it will work the paint into the carpet pile.

- For *latex* paint, which is usually water-soluble, use detergent solution followed by ammonia solution, if needed.

- For *oil-based* paint, use specific solvent mentioned on the label. If there's no information on the label, apply paint thinner or turpentine. Pretest first. If stain remains, work on it with detergent solution, then ammonia solution. Rinse with warm water and blot dry.

PET STAINS: We love our pets, but hate their messes! Get to these ASAP.

"Solids"—Remove solid material first. Use a detergent solution. Rinse and blot. Apply vinegar solution; rinse and blot dry.

"Liquids"—Soak up all liquids first! Rinse area with cool water and blot. Next, apply a warm detergent solution. Follow with a vinegar solution, blotting between each. Rinse and blot dry.

Note: Although many professionals suggest using an ammonia solution, I personally don't care to because it smells similar to urine and may encourage your pet to commit repeat offenses! Also, enzyme-based pet stain and odor removers are good to have on hand.

"RED" STAIN: A difficult stain to get out, try these hints by using SMALL amounts and blotting frequently, so the carpet doesn't get too wet. Work from the outer edge of the stain to the center. Test first on a hidden area to make sure the carpet is colorfast. Use solutions below and rinse the stained area with water and blot dry. Try these hints, until one works:

- Mix 1 teaspoon mild, colorless dishwashing liquid in a cup of lukewarm water. Blot and rinse.

- Combine ½ cup water with 1 tablespoon clear household ammonia.

- Apply a solution of ⅓ cup white household vinegar mixed with ⅔ cup water.

After trying these solutions, if the stain is still there, it just may be permanent. You may be able to cut the stain out of the carpet and replace with a plug, if you have extra carpet. (See HOW TO PATCH CARPET, page 108.)

RED WINE: As soon as possible, blot up liquid with paper towels. Work from the outside of the stain to the inside, dabbing on a mixture of ½ teaspoon mild white dishwashing liquid with 1 cup lukewarm water. If this doesn't work, combine ⅓ cup white vinegar and ⅔ cup water. Dab on. Blot with water and then pat dry.

Carpets, Rugs, and Floors

RUST: Try a paste of lemon juice and salt, or vinegar and salt. Let sit for a time, then rinse off and blot dry.

SHOE POLISH: Use dry-cleaning solvent, then detergent solution, then an ammonia solution, blotting between each. Rinse and blot dry. Bleach out persistent stains with 3 to 5 percent hydrogen peroxide. Pretest first.

SOFT DRINKS: Use cold detergent solution, blot. Apply vinegar solution then blot. Rinse and blot until dry.

STICKY RESIDUE: Gummed name stickers and labels leave a sticky gunk, which can be removed by dabbing with denatured alcohol or dry-cleaning solvent.

TOMATO SAUCE/KETCHUP: Use cool water and rinse well. Apply a cool detergent solution, rinse and blot. Follow with an ammonia solution. Rinse and blot. If any traces still linger, use 3 to 5 percent hydrogen peroxide to remove.

TONER CARTRIDGE: Get to it ASAP. Cleaning depends on the type of cartridge and ink you have.

- Powdered ink: Vacuum it up. Hold the vacuum attachment above the stain. Don't let it touch the fiber because that might grind it further in the carpet. Apply a spotting or cleaning agent (carpet cleaner) with foaming action to lift up the ink. Blot and repeat until it's gone. Rinse and blot with water to remove the detergent or cleaning agent residue.

- Liquid ink: Blot up as much as possible with dry toweling and be sure to work from the outer edge toward the center of the spill. Put alcohol (isopropyl) carefully on a clean white cotton towel. CAUTION: Do not pour alcohol directly onto the carpet. Blot the stain. Repeat until no ink is being transferred onto the towel. If there's still a stain, you can also apply household hydrogen peroxide to a white cotton towel and blot the stain. Rinse thoroughly. Allow to dry overnight.

VOMIT: Remove solid residue and rinse. Use a warm detergent solution, then move on to an ammonia solution and finally to a vinegar solution, rinsing and blotting between each application. Rinse and blot dry (See page 114.).

PART FIVE

All Around the House

This final section covers everything inside and outside the house, from aluminum siding to appliances and windows to woodwork. Of course, many of the products and cleaning methods that I've recommended in the clothing and carpet sections will apply here. Isn't that good news! But still, there are countless items, fabrics, and circumstances unique to your home that just may need a special Heloise touch. Hope this helps!

Having the right tools for the job is still the first step in winning the stain battle. So, here follows the READ ME FIRST section with my suggestions and those of our many knowledgeable experts.

3 Steps to Choosing the Right Cleaning Product

Our friends at The Soap and Detergent Association offer this helpful advice:

1. Check Out the Soils and Surfaces

The first thing to consider in any cleaning task is: What am I trying to get rid of? Is there grease on the stove, mildew on the shower door or do you have hard water that leaves mineral deposits on bathroom and kitchen fixtures? Identifying the dirt you see—or maybe don't see, in the case of germs—is the first step in determining the type of cleaning product you need.

Now look at where the dirt is located. In other words, what type of surface is soiled? Today's beautiful surfaces offer many options in home décor, but they also require a bit of thought about how to safely clean them.

2. Consider Your Own Cleaning Needs

Are you a once-a-month, bucket-wielding cleaner who likes to use dilutable powders or liquids to tackle the whole house? Or do you prefer quick, frequent cleanups using spray cleaners? Do you need the heavy-duty strength of a powdered cleanser? Do you have young children and need to disinfect surfaces regularly? Taking a moment to think about your lifestyle, cleaning needs and preferences will help you decide among the various product types: abrasive cleaners, nonabrasive cleaners, disinfectant and other specialty cleaners; and product forms: sprays, gels, foams, dilutable powders and liquids. There's a wide variety of cleaning product options to meet your needs and make your job easier.

3. Read the Label . . .

On the cleaning product:

Product labels are your best source of information for choosing a cleaner. Mildew remover . . . oven cleaner . . . glass cleaner . . . the name itself usually says exactly what the product will do. And if the name doesn't tell you, the back of the label will explain the types of soils the product is formulated to remove and the surfaces it should or shouldn't be used on. Labels provide just about everything we need to know about a cleaning product and its safe and effective use.

On surfaces and appliances:

Fiberglass, no-wax floors, countertop surfaces, ceramic glass cooktops—all have their own characteristics and cleaning requirements. Most surface and appliance manufacturers give instructions for cleaning their products . . . usually on a tag or sticker attached to the product. Or, contact your retailer or the manufacturer for care instructions. These are your best guides to caring for and cleaning new purchases.

Types of Household Cleaners

The following guidelines are provided by The Soap and Detergent Association. Household cleaners are available as liquids, gels, powders, solids, sheets and pads for use on painted, plastic, metal, porcelain, glass and other surfaces, and on washable floor coverings. Because no single product can provide optimum performance on all surfaces and soils, a broad range of products has been formulated to clean efficiently and easily. While all-purpose cleaners are intended for more general use, others work best under highly specialized conditions.

Abrasive cleaners remove heavy accumulations of soil often found in small areas. The abrasive action is provided by small mineral or metal particles, fine steel wool, copper or nylon particles. Some also disinfect.

All-purpose cleaners penetrate and loosen soil, soften water and prevent soil from redepositing on the cleaned surface. Some also disinfect.

Drain openers unclog kitchen and bathroom drains. They work by producing heat to melt fats, breaking them down into simpler substances that can be rinsed away, or by oxidizing hair and other materials. Some use bacteria to prevent grease build-up, which leads to drain clogging.

Glass and multi-surface cleaners remove soils from a variety of smooth surfaces. They shine surfaces without streaking.

Glass cleaners loosen and dissolve oily soils found on glass, and dry quickly without streaking.

Metal cleaners remove soils and polish metalware. Tarnish, the oxidation of metal, is the principal soil found on metalware. Some products also protect cleaned metalware against rapid re-tarnishing.

Oven cleaners remove burned-on grease and other food soils from oven walls. These cleaners are thick so the product will cling to vertical oven surfaces.

Rug shampoos and upholstery cleaners dissolve oily and greasy soils and hold them in suspension for removal. Some also treat surfaces to repel soil.

Specialty cleaners are designed for the soil conditions found on specific surfaces, such as glass, tile, metal, ovens, carpets and upholstery, toilet bowls and in drains.

Toilet bowl cleaners prevent or remove stains caused by hard water and rust deposits, and maintain a clean and pleasant-smelling bowl. Some products also disinfect.

Tub, tile and sink cleaners remove normal soils found on bathroom surfaces as well as hard-water deposits, soap scum, rust stains, and/or mildew and mold. Some also treat surfaces to retard soiling; some also disinfect.

All Around the House Stains A-to-Z

AIR CONDITIONING/EXHAUST-FAN GRILLS/CEILING FANS: Wipe often with full-strength vinegar to clean and dust. This also helps to keep fresh air circulation.

ALUMINUM POTS AND PANS: To eliminate discoloring, fill pot or pan with water; add 1 tablespoon cream of tartar for each quart of water used. Boil for around 10 minutes. Pour out. Wash and rinse as usual. Or, put 1 cup vinegar and 1 cup water in the pot and boil. Wash as usual, rinse and dry.

ALUMINUM SCREENS: To clean up pitted frames, remove screens and treat outdoors with a rag dipped in kerosene. Rub both sides of the screen and frame. Wipe off carefully. This acts as a rust inhibitor for older screens. CAUTION: Kerosene is flammable.

Safety First Do's And Don't's

Household cleaning products are safe when used and stored according to the directions on the label. Follow the label directions carefully, and if you have any questions, call the toll-free number found on most product labels. Here are some simple precautions to help prevent accidents from occurring:

DO:
- *Read and follow label directions for proper use, storage and disposal.*
- *Store cleaning products away from food and out of the reach of children or pets.*
- *Store products in their original containers and keep the original label intact. Product use and storage, disposal instructions, precautions and first aid instructions vary according to their ingredients. It can be dangerous to use a product incorrectly or to follow the wrong emergency procedures.*
- *Put cleaning products away immediately after removing the amount needed for the job. This will limit accessibility to young children and help prevent accidental spills.*
- *Keep buckets containing cleaning solutions out of the reach of young children.*
- *Properly close all containers, especially those with child-resistant caps.*

DON'T:
- *Mix cleaning products. Products, which are safe when used alone, can sometimes cause dangerous fumes if mixed with other products.*
- *Reuse an empty household cleaning product container for any other purpose. The label instructions and precautions for the original product may be inaccurate or dangerous if used for a different product.*

Courtesy of The Soap and Detergent Association

Do not light up anything while doing this task. Store flammables, clearly marked, in a cool place, away from ANY heat source.

ALUMINUM SIDING: To remove dirt, attach a car-washing brush to your hose and rinse the house about every 6 months.

APPLIANCES I: CAUTION: Always unplug electrical appliances before cleaning. Clean plastic-coated with a nonabrasive, all-purpose cleaner. Rinse well and dry with a soft, clean cloth. CAUTION: Do not use abrasive cleansers because they may scratch the plastic.

APPLIANCES II: You can wax the outside of enamel refrigerators, freezers, washers and dryers with car wax. It will help to erase fine-line scratches and also make them shine.

BARBECUE GRILL: Spritz a healthy amount of white vinegar over scrunched up aluminum foil and scrub the grill vigorously to clean off dirty gunk. Or, use commercial cleaners.

BATHTUB: CAUTION: Do NOT use any abrasive cleanser on fiberglass (or porcelain tiles) because it could permanently scratch the tub, making it even more difficult to clean. While there are cleaners made especially for fiberglass, you also can use cheap hair shampoo (without conditioners) or liquid dishwashing detergent to clean it. A nylon scrubbie will do the job on stubborn stains. To prevent a buildup, rinse and dry after each use and every 6 months apply a top-quality auto paste wax to the sides, inside and out. CAUTION: Do NOT wax the bottom of the tub because you could slip and do damage to yourself.

All Around the House

BATHTUB: To get rid of rust rings on the ledges, such as those left behind from a metal shaving cream can, make a paste of cream of tartar and hydrogen peroxide. Rub a small amount into the stain with an old toothbrush and keep scrubbing until gone. If this does not work, use a powdered cleanser with oxalic acid (see the label). But follow the directions exactly. CAUTION: NEVER use bleach because it will speed up the rusting process.

Reader Letter of Laughter

"I grabbed the can of cleanser out of the grocery bag and headed to the bathroom to give this new product a try. I slid the plastic lid around exposing an outlined oval. Using the bottom of my toothbrush, I pushed in the oval and turned the cover until I could sprinkle the contents into the basin. Instead of the customary blue color, it was yellow and had a very strange odor. It was only then that I looked at the label to discover that I was cleaning with Parmesan cheese!

BIRDBATH: If the concrete is slimy inside, it's probably algae. Empty all the water then pour in a bit of household bleach diluted with water. Rub and scrub over the entire surface. Rinse several times with clear water to get rid of all the bleach residue; then refill with fresh water.

BLENDER: Rinse out with water, then fill halfway with water and add a drop of liquid dishwashing liquid. Put lid on and turn on low to agitate. Rinse well.

BRASS I: To remove tarnish from brass fireplace tools, buff with a fine emery cloth, found at hardware stores.

BRASS II: To remove tarnish from a lacquered item, wipe off surface with a damp cloth. CAUTION: Do NOT use cleaner of any kind. If item is unlacquered, dissolve 1 teaspoon salt with 1 cup white vinegar; add flour to make a paste. Apply to brass and leave on for 10 minutes. Rinse item extremely well. Polish dry. The best bet is commercial cleaners specially formulated for cleaning brass.

BRICKS: If a small area of fireplace bricks gets sooty, press light-colored children's modeling dough on the brick and lift away. For a larger area, dip a scrub brush into a container of full-strength white household vinegar. Start from the bottom up, cleaning SMALL sections at a time. It may take several tries to remove completely. Note: If brick is very old or in poor condition, test modeling dough in a small spot first to make sure it doesn't pull off any of the surface. Or, use a mixture of half laundry bleach and half water put into a spray bottle. Spritz bricks and clean with a soft-bristled brush. Rinse with water.

BURNED FOOD: If food has burned onto the bottom of your cooking pot, soak the pot in full-strength vinegar for 30 minutes. Scrub and wash well. Or, add 3 tablespoons baking soda with enough water to cover the bottom. Simmer until gunk comes off.

BURN MARKS: Burns marks on *laminated countertops* cannot be removed. Patch the burned area if you have a matching piece of laminate. Or, if possible, cut out the area and replace with a cutting board or decorative tile.

CANDLE SOOT ON WHITE STUCCO CEILING: Mix a TINY amount of water with the powdered cleaner trisodium phosphate (TSP), which is available at home-improvement and paint stores, to make a paste. Test a small hidden area first. Blot (don't over-wet!) the paste on the stained area only. This may not work on painted surfaces. Check with your local paint or hardware store for specific recommendations for specific paints.

CAR STEERING WHEEL: If it becomes gummy, treat with a pre-wash spray. CAUTION: Do NOT use on fancy leather or fur. Apply spray to a sponge or cloth, rub wheel, let stand for a minute or two. Then rub with a plastic scrubbie. Rinse well and dry off.

CEILING: To get rid of water stains, do NOT just paint over them because they'll be back to bleed through the paint. First, find out the source of the leak and make SURE it's fixed. Then, cover the stain with clear varnish or a product sold in paint stores to prevent stains from coming through. Let dry completely. It may be a good idea to apply 2 coats of varnish of the product before painting.

CERAMIC TILES (unglazed): Use an all-purpose household cleaner on UNGLAZED tiles but be sure it is not a high-alkaline cleaner or citrus based. Allow it to stand for 5 to 10 minutes, so it can work. Then scrub with a nylon-bristled brush. Rinse well. Commercial ceramic tile cleaners are also available.

CERAMIC TILES (glazed): Clean with an all-purpose cleaner or a commercial tile cleaner. For the crystalline tiles, use a mild soap detergent. NEVER use citrus based cleaners or alkaline cleaners. CAUTION: Citrus fruit and foods containing acid may take the finish off the crystalline tiles. When purchasing tiles, ask the distributor for the proper care and any cautions.

CHINA: For some marks, rub with baking soda or cover the piece with liquid or powdered dishwasher detergent and water. Let it sit for several hours or overnight.

CHOPPING-BLOCK COUNTERTOPS: Scrub surfaces with soap and water or a paste of baking soda and water. You can also deodorize by sprinkling the cutting board with salt and then scrubbing with half a lemon or vinegar on a sponge. Be aware that cuts and crevices can hold bacteria. Occasionally, disinfect the counter or chopping block with a solution of 2 to 3 tablespoons bleach to a quart of water. Rinse surface very well. Let dry. Recoat surface with a thin layer of mineral oil (NOT vegetable oil) and allow it to soak for 30 minutes.

CHROME: To remove spots from taps, etc., put tissues over the fixtures and pour full-strength vinegar over them. Let sit for several minutes. Sponge with soap and water; rinse well. Polish with a soft cloth or towel.

CLAY POTS: The noticeable white rings that appear on pots both outside and inside are usually caused by a salt buildup. Wipe pots with a cloth soaked in undiluted vinegar.

COFFEEMAKER: It's best to wash a glass coffeepot after each use with soap and hot water so coffee oils don't build up to create a bitter taste. Run full-strength white vinegar through a normal brew cycle to clean the machine too. Then run several cycles of hot water to clear out the vinegar. CAUTION: After running vinegar through the cycle, don't put the machine on autopilot and put coffee in by mistake!

COFFEE STAINS: To get rid of stains in cups and mugs, rub in the inside with a mixture of half salt and half white vinegar (or baking soda and hydrogen peroxide) then wash as usual.

All Around the House

COMPACT DISK: Wipe, in a straight line from the center to the edge, with a dry, soft, lint-free cloth. To get rid of greasy fingerprints, which affect playing performance, rinse under running cool water (avoid getting the label wet) and blot dry with a lint-free cloth. Commercial cleaning kits may do the best job. CAUTION: Do NOT clean CDs with abrasive cleaners or solvent.

COMPUTERS: Unplug equipment first. Vacuum around your computer and all related equipment often.

- To clean the screen, dust with a lint-free cloth or use commercial cleaner pads. Let the screen air-dry. CAUTION: Never use window cleaners or any spray or liquid cleaner on your computer monitor screen.

- To clean the keyboard, wipe with a lint-free cloth. If needed, spray antistatic cleaning fluid on a soft cloth to wipe the keyboard. Turn the keyboard upside down and gently shake it to dislodge anything that might be lurking inside. CAUTION: Do NOT spray anything wet on the keyboard. If you do spill a clear liquid on the keyboard, unplug it and turn upside down to dry. If you spill sugared substances or anything sticky on it, take to a service person immediately.

- To dust the printer, open it up and use a clean long-handled soft brush to get rid of any dust inside.

COOKIE SHEETS I: To get rid of greasy buildup on regular metal sheets, elbow grease with a scouring powder or fine steel wool should remove it. Or, try oven cleaner. CAUTION: Do NOT use this method on nonstick pans.

COOKIE SHEETS II: To clean up nonstick pans, soak in hot, sudsy water and use a nylon scrubber. NEVER use abrasive cleaners or steel wool. Do NOT use metal utensils on nonstick surfaces; use wooden or plastic tools. Do NOT put nonstick pans into the dishwasher. Read manufacturer's care and cleaning instructions for your particular brand.

COPPER: If the item is lacquered, wipe off surface with a damp cloth; do NOT use cleaners. If item is unlacquered, drizzle vinegar directly on the object and follow by sprinkling salt from a saltshaker over that and scrub. Or: Sprinkle salt on the sponge and drizzle vinegar over the sponge and then scrub away. Wipe with a paper towel. Rinse well and dry thoroughly. There are commercial cleaners designed specifically to clean copper also.

CORK FLOORING/WALL COVERING: Because cork is porous, use a floor wax on a regular basis to protect the surface. You can add a sealer as a protective coating. Follow directions carefully. Avoid using water on cork. Wipe up spills ASAP with a damp sponge.

COUNTERTOPS: Some difficult stains on laminated countertops can be lightened with a paste of baking soda and lemon juice. Let paste dry; then wipe up with a damp sponge. If that doesn't work on stains such as indelible ink, marking pens and newsprint, try using a little denatured alcohol on a cotton swab. Be careful since some solvents are extremely flammable. Follow directions on the containers. CAUTION: Do not use acid (citrus cleaners) or alkaline-based cleaners for general daily cleaning. They may corrode, etch, and permanently damage laminates by discoloring them. If you accidentally damage the surface with scouring powder or an abrasive pad, restore the shiny surface temporarily with mineral oil or silicone car polish.

CRAYON ON BLACKBOARD: Use an oil-based lubricating spray to remove marks without damaging the blackboard. Test first on a small spot. Spray and let set for several minutes. Wipe off with a clean dry cloth. You may need to repeat to remove. Then add several drops of liquid dishwashing detergent to warm water. With a clean sponge, wipe down the board with a circular motion to remove any oily residue. Rinse well with warm water. Dry with a clean cloth. Don't use until completely dry.

CRAYON ON CAR UPHOLSTERY: To remove melted crayon, scrape off what you can with a spoon. Apply lubricating oil spray (used for squeaks) to lightly cover the stain. Do NOT over-saturate. Allow it to set for 2 or 3 minutes. Use a toothbrush to gently scrub the area, working from the outside to the inside of the stain, so it won't spread. Blot with paper towels then apply a bit more spray and a couple drops of dishwashing liquid. (Test soap on a hidden area for colorfastness.) Work in with the toothbrush. Use a dampened sponge to get rid of all traces of soap and spray. Repeat if you have to.

CRAYON ON PAINTED WALLS/WASHABLE WALLPAPER: Spray a multi-purpose lubricating oil on a sponge or paper towel—do not let it drip on the floor—and apply to the stain. Gently wipe with a paper towel or clean white cloth. Dry-cleaning solvent will also work well. If the mark remains, pour a bit of baking soda on a damp sponge and gently rub in a circular motion to remove. If there is any lubricant residue left behind, dampen a sponge with a mixture of several drops of mild dishwashing liquid to 1 cup water. Squeeze extra liquid out of the sponge and apply to stain. Rinse sponge and go over area. Dry with a clean cloth.

CRYSTAL DECANTER: If dishwasher detergent and hot water don't get rid of the stains, fill the decanter with full-strength warm to hot white vinegar and soak overnight or for several days, depending on the stain. Scrub with a bottle brush. Wash and rinse as usual.

DISHWASHER: To remove brownish-orange stains, use a lemon or orange powdered breakfast drink. It's the citric acid that works. Put 1 or 2 tablespoons, but no detergent, in the dishwasher cups. Run the dishwasher through the wash cycle. Repeat until all stains are removed. It should look almost new.

DOOR TRACKS, SLIDING GLASS: Clean stains by spraying or pouring full-strength vinegar into the door tracks. Let it sit for a bit. Rinse out with water and dry.

DRIED EGG OR MILK: To make getting these stains off your dishes easier, soak them in cold water first. Hot water may actually make the stain harder to remove!

DRIVEWAY OIL: If the stains are new, sprinkle CLAY-TYPE cat litter or baking soda over the spots. Use a stiff-bristle brush to get the litter into the driveway so it will absorb the oil. Leave on overnight and then sweep up. You may have to repeat several times. If the stains are old, commercial cleaners are available at home-improvement or auto stores. Finally, renting a high-powered pressure spray may work.

ELECTRICAL APPLIANCE CORDS: To remove food splatters off cords, first unplug appliance, then dip a sponge into warm sudsy water and run along cord. Do not wet the plug. Dry with a clean cloth.

ENAMELWARE: Can be put in the dishwasher, but do not scour with powders or steel wool.

FLOOR: A dull film on a *no-wax* floor may occur if it has not been rinsed properly after using detergents or floor cleaners. A sticky film can trap dirt. Check with the manufacturer to be certain that you are using the right cleaning agent.

FLOOR: To get rid of the dull film on a *waxed floor*, mop with a mixture of 1 cup fabric softener in a half pail of water between washings.

FREEZER: To clean and remove stains, take everything out of the freezer and wipe down with a solution of liquid dishwashing detergent and water or baking soda and water.

FURNITURE: To clean leather use a paste soap or foam designed for cleaning leather. Follow the manufacturer's care instructions.

FURNITURE, CABINETS, WOOD PANELING: To get rid of shallow scratches, marks, or discolorations, use paste shoe polish or a crayon. Try dark brown on dark wood and tan on lighter wood.

GARAGE FLOOR: To get out oil stains, pour 1 cup baking soda on small freshly made oil spills. Sprinkle with ½ cup water and scrub. Rinse well and mop dry. Or, use CLAY-TYPE cat litter as an alternative to the baking soda, particularly on large spills. Pour it over the oil and grind it in with your feet. Leave overnight; then sweep up. Wash area with detergent and water; rinse well.

If these do not do the job, douse the spots/stains with full-strength laundry bleach and wipe up any excess with rags. CAUTION: Wear protective gloves when using bleach.

For old spills, scrape off all residue with an old knife or paint scraper. Cover the spills with clay-type cat litter or sawdust, grind in with your feet. The stains should be absorbed into the litter or sawdust. Sweep up and wash the area with detergent, rinse and mop dry.

GLASS COOKTOPS: Let cooktop cool before cleaning. Use a non-abrasive sponge or clean cloth. Apply a paste of baking soda and water to it and wipe surface or use a ceramic glass cleaner. Do NOT use cleaners that contain bleach or ammonia. NOTE: Always follow the owner's manual for your appliance.

GLASS COOKWARE: To get rid of burned-on grease, spray the cookware with oven cleaner and let stand for 30 minutes. Wash and rinse well.

GLASSES I: To try to eliminate foggy film, soak in warm to hot, full strength vinegar and then scrub with a brush or plastic scrub-

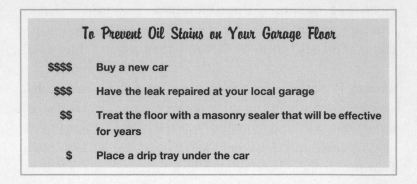

To Prevent Oil Stains on Your Garage Floor

$$$$	Buy a new car
$$$	Have the leak repaired at your local garage
$$	Treat the floor with a masonry sealer that will be effective for years
$	Place a drip tray under the car

bie. If the filmy coating persists, the glasses are etched (little scratches). Etching cannot be removed, sad to say.

GLASSES II: To prevent hard water spots from forming on glasses in the dishwasher, be sure to use the right amount of dishwasher detergent. More IS NOT better! Adding a rinsing agent will help make the water run off the dishes faster and speed the drying process, which also helps to prevent spots from forming. When hand-washing, don't air-dry glasses (especially fine crystal), dry with a soft, lint-free towel.

GLASS-TOP COFFEE TABLE: A permanent marker stain should come off with regular glass cleaner and some elbow grease. If that doesn't do it, moisten a cotton ball with full strength household isopropyl (rubbing) alcohol.

GRAVY STAINS (on a tablecloth): As soon as you see a spill, spoon up as much of it as possible. Blot the stain with paper towels. Put the tablecloth into a sink and soak with a mixture of one teaspoon of a mild, colorless detergent to each cup of lukewarm water. If the stain is still there, put a full-strength liquid laundry detergent on the fabric, rub it well and then launder as you normally do. (See GREASE following.)

GREASE (on a tablecloth): Spoon off any blobs of grease. Then sprinkle cornstarch or artificial sweetener or talcum powder over the stain to absorb it. When absorbed, brush powder off. Use a prewash spray and wash in the hottest water safe for the fabric. Read the care label. Before putting into the dryer, check stain to make sure it's gone.

GROUT: Clean grout in kitchen or bathroom tiles with a mild bleach solution, about 2 tablespoons bleach to a quart of water. A cotton swab or toothbrush is a handy applicator for the bleach solution.

HARDWOOD FLOORS I: Chair legs or furniture feet may mar hardwood floors. You may be able to minimize the damage by filling the dents with shellac or clear nail polish. Apply self-adhesive-backed moleskin to the bottom of chair legs to prevent this damage.

HARDWOOD FLOORS II: Wax, polyurethane or other liquids can seep through the protective finish on the floor and soak into the grain of the wood causing *black spots* or dark stained areas. Wipe up spills immediately or the floor can be damaged so it will need refinishing. If black spots are not stained too deep, they can be removed.

On a *waxed* floor, rub the spots gently with fine sandpaper or very fine steel wool. That will lighten the area, so it will have to be re-stained and waxed to match the rest of the floor.

On a floor with a *polyurethane* finish, the black spots may be due to cracked polyurethane, caused by age or impact. Strip off the polyurethane and sand the spots. Restain to an even color, if you have to. Apply fresh coats of polyurethane.

INK: To get ink stains out of *leather furniture*, dip a cotton swab into a bit of rubbing alcohol or patent leather cleaner and carefully dab at the stain. Then wipe with a damp sponge and recondition the leather.

IRON: To get rid of the stains on the bottom, first turn off the iron, UNPLUG it, and let it get cold. To remove starch or synthetic fiber buildup or icky brown gunk, wipe the bottom with a cloth soaked in diluted white vinegar. Repeat if you have to. Also, iron cleaner (in a tube) is worth having on hand.

LAWN CHAIRS: To remove stains from white plastic chairs, use a solution of ¾ cup household bleach and 1 tablespoon powdered or liquid laundry detergent with one gallon warm water. (Test solution on a small hidden area to make sure plastic won't discolor.) Wearing rubber gloves, scrub with a soft-bristled brush or sponge. Let mixture stay on the chair for 5 to 15 minutes. Then rinse well.

LEATHER-TOPPED FURNITURE: To remedy drink spills, first blot up. Then, cover the leather with saddle soap and let it dry totally. If there is a white mark still remaining, match a color of scuff-type liquid polish to the area to see if you can disguise the spill mark. If the piece is antique and valuable, talk with leather experts or ask about commercial leather polishes sold in furniture stores.

LINEN NAPKINS/TABLECLOTHS: To remove stains from white damask, try dabbing 3 percent hydrogen peroxide with a cotton tip and wait for 24 hours to see if the stain comes off. If they are permanently stained you can dye them or have them professionally done.

LIPSTICK: To remove lipstick from a table napkin, place paper towels under the stained area. Dab a bit of rubbing alcohol on the stained area and gently rub. Keep blotting until the stain is gone. Then launder the napkins as usual.

MARBLE: Marble needs to be treated with care. You can clean it with this home-style solution: Mix 1 tablespoon mild liquid dishwashing detergent (that you hand-wash dishes with) with 1 quart warm water and apply to a small area at a time with a sponge to clean. Rinse the marble completely to remove any and all soap residue. (According to the Marble Institute of America, a buildup could damage the stone.) Buff dry with a soft cloth so water will not be left standing; never allow to air dry because water will leave stains.

Do not use any acidic cleaners, such as lemon, vinegar, bathroom or kitchen cleansers, on marble because they will eat into the surface.

In the bathroom, if you are using alcohol-based products, such as aftershave lotion or perfume, around the marble counters, put water over the surface area first, so the alcohol will not come in direct contact with it; the alcohol will evaporate instead. The reason? Alcohol can be reactive and cause etching of the surface. DON'T use hair dyes in marble sinks or over marble counters because the dye could cause permanent damage to the color of the stone. You are asking for trouble!

MATTRESSES: To get rid of urine stains, first soak up all the moisture with towels ASAP. Apply upholstery shampoo to the stain and rub from the outside of the stain to the inside to avoid making the stain larger. Or: Sponge the area with a solution of half water and half white vinegar. Dry with towels. You may have to repeat this process because the outer ring's stain could be harder to remove than the stain itself. Rinse well. Put the mattress in the sun to dry, if possible. When dry, spray affected area with a deodorant spray. (See also URINE in the STINKS section, page 35 and PET STAINS in the CARPET section, page 114.)

MICROWAVE: To remove stains, clean up splattered food right after cooking so it won't stick. But if it does, add 2 tablespoons of either baking soda or lemon juice into 1 cup water in a 4-cup microwave-safe bowl. Allow the mixture to boil in the oven for about 5 minutes. Let set 15 minutes to cool. The steam will condense on the inside walls. Then just wipe off the walls, inside of the door and don't forget the door seals.

MILDEW ON HOUSE EXTERIOR: Wash affected area with a mixture of 1 quart bleach to every gallon of non-ammonia detergent solution. Let dry. Note: Put plastic drop cloths down, so no drops of bleach will hit grass or shrubbery or anything else that could be discolored.

MINIBLINDS: To clean greasy metal miniblinds, wipe with a solution of a teaspoon of mild liquid detergent to 1 quart warm water.

MIRRORS: Make bathroom mirrors sparkle by polishing with a cloth dipped into a borax and water solution. Wipe dry with paper toweling or an old nylon stocking. Bathroom mirrors will not steam up if you run an inch of cold water in the bathtub or sink before you add hot water.

MIRRORS: Remove spots with a homemade glass-cleaning solution of 2 cups water with 1 cup isopropyl rubbing alcohol (70 percent) and 1 tablespoon household ammonia. Pour into a clean pump-spray bottle.

Or: For a fast cleanup, pour a bit of vinegar on a paper towel and wipe.

To get rid of hairspray residue, rubbing alcohol will do the job.

CAUTION: Always put cleaning product onto a clean cloth and then apply to mirror; that way you've kept the cleaning product away from the frame so it's not damaged.

NEEDLE: To clean a rusty needle, push it through a soap-filled steel wool pad several times.

OLIVE OIL: For olive oil–based stains on a tablecloth or napkin, sprinkle any artificial sweetener (from packets) over the oil stain. Let set to absorb the oil. It may pull all of it up. On washable material, apply liquid laundry detergent directly on the spot then wash as usual in hot water. It may take several times.

OVEN I: Do NOT use any cleaning aid in a *continuous- or self-cleaning* oven; it could damage or ruin the finish. Instead use liquid detergent and water or window cleaner instead to wipe up spills. Use a damp sponge to wipe up the ash after cleaning.

All Around the House

OVEN II: If the oven is really dirty, wear rubber gloves and have plenty of air circulation when you use commercial oven cleaners. Follow directions carefully. Do not spray the electrical connections, heating elements or lightbulbs. If the oven is only mildly stained, sprinkle baking soda onto a damp cloth and scrub. To make this onerous task easier, clean up spills right after they happen. Pour salt on burned food, let the oven cool and wipe clean.

OVEN III: To remove melted plastic from the electric oven— don't ask, it's happened to many people—put a bag of ice on top of the melted plastic to chill it, thus making it more brittle. Gently and very carefully use a razor-blade scraper to lift off the plastic puddle. Note: This will not hurt an interior porcelain finish.

OVEN IV: To clean the racks, remove them from oven and take outside. Put them inside a big heavy-duty plastic trash bag; spray them with an oven cleaner or, put 2 tablespoons ammonia in and close the bag tightly. Let soak overnight. The next day, spray off with a hose (do not let residue run into plants or onto any surface that could be damaged). If any spots or stains remain, use a scrub brush to get them off.

PATIO UMBRELLA: To get rid of the mildew, use a solution of 1 gallon water, ¾ cup liquid household bleach and a squirt of liquid dishwashing detergent. (CAUTION: Avoid using detergents that should not be combined with chlorine bleach. Check the label.) Open umbrella outdoors and lay on its side. Put on glove and old clothes and use a soft-bristled brush. Test a bit of the solution under the umbrella for colorfastness. Then scrub each section of the umbrella. Rinse thoroughly with a hose and dry any metal parts. Note: Do NOT use on acrylic prints because bleach will fade colors. Read care label.

PILLOWS: Read care labels. Many pillows can be washed on gentle cycle. Always dissolve detergent in the water first; then add pillows. If the stuffing is foam rubber, air-dry only. Some feather pillows can be washed but have to be placed in the dryer. Fluff pillows as they dry. CAUTION: Check the seams carefully or you'll have feathers everywhere!

PLASTIC CONTAINER: To remove stubborn tomato stains, start with baking soda. Put a small amount on a damp cloth and rub the stains. If stains remain, soak the container for about a minute in a solution of ⅛ cup of liquid bleach and 1 quart water. (Keep solution weak so it does not ruin the finish on the plastic.) Wash and rinse well. These stains may be removed by setting the plastic container in the sun for several hours.

PLASTIC PET TOYS: Put them into a solution of baking soda and water. Scrub to remove yucky stuff. Rinse and dry.

PLASTIC SHOWER CURTAIN OR TABLECLOTH: Using the delicate cycle, wash in warm water with a couple of bath towels for scrubbing action. Dry on warm and take out after 5 minutes or so.

All Around the House

PLASTIC TOYS: Get rid of grime by making a solution of 4 tablespoons baking soda to 1 quart water. Wipe it on toys and then wipe off with a clean, dry cloth. This works well for molded plastic furniture too.

PLAY PUTTY (on fabric sofa): Use isoamyl acetate (banana oil), which is available at pharmacies. In a well-ventilated area, pour a little isoamyl acetate onto the putty. Then add a bit more. Scrape off putty with a dull-edged knife. The isoamyl acetate should evaporate and not leave a stain, but always test in a hidden spot before using.

PORCELAIN SINKS (colored): To clean colored porcelain, use a mild liquid dishwashing detergent, baking soda or vinegar. Do NOT use any kind of bleach on a colored porcelain sink; it will fade the color. Don't use abrasive cleaners either.

PORCELAIN SINKS (white): On white or light-colored sinks, make a solution of ¾ cup chlorine bleach to 1 gallon of water. Let set for ONLY 5 minutes and rinse well. Note: Let everyone in the house know what's happening and keep children and pets away.

PORCELAIN TILES: Mix a solution of equal amounts of vinegar and water and apply to the tiles. Scrub with a nylon-bristled brush. Rinse well. Don't use on crystalline tiles!

POTS: To clean a stained enamel pot, fill it with water and add ⅛ cup of bleach. Allow the pot to soak for 10 minutes then wash as usual. If stains are really stubborn, you may have to repeat this process several times. To avoid this problem, clean pots well after each use.

RANGE BURNER DRIP BOWLS: It's best to clean them after use if needed with dishwashing detergent and water. Scrub with a plastic scouring pad, rinse and dry. For heavy stains, soak a paper towel in ammonia and put it on the stained area. Then scrub with a plastic scouring pad. Do not use abrasive cleansers.

RANGE-HOOD FILTER: If the filter can be removed and will fit, wash in the dishwasher. If you have to wash the filter by hand, try an ammonia-based window cleaner or detergent specifically formulated to remove grease. Apply the cleaner, let soak, rinse. Repeat if necessary.

RANGE TOP: Wipe off with hot soapy water right after a spill. Harsh scouring powders can scratch chrome; use metal polishes made for chromium.

RECORDS: To clean vinyl records, it may be best to use a commercial kit, but you can try this method: Holding the record by the edges, rinse both sides with a stream of cold tap water. Try to keep the label dry. Squirt a bit of mild liquid detergent (no bar soap) on your wet fingertips. Rub around record with the grooves and not across them. Rinse well and let dry. Do not use a towel or lint-producing fabric. Get a cloth designed for wiping records.

REFRIGERATORS/APPLIANCES: Use a solution of half vinegar and half water on an old clean terry towel to wipe away smears and finger marks.

All Around the House

RUBBER HANDLES (on appliances): They may get sticky, but don't use strong cleaners on them. To prevent tacky buildup wipe handles clean daily but for stubborn dirt, try one of these methods:

- Mix baking soda and a bit of water together. Rub the paste on the handles (not on black though) to clean.

- Mix mild liquid soap and water. Apply with a clean sponge.

- Use a mild spray cleaner.

SCREWS AND BOLTS: Soak rusty or corroded nuts and bolts in vinegar overnight or longer. Vinegar also can loosen up the mechanism in a padlock.

SCUFF MARKS ON FLOORS: Shoe scuff marks on resilient floors can be taken off by simply rubbing them with a pencil eraser or dry paper towel. Believe me. It works!

SCUFF MARKS ON NO-WAX KITCHEN FLOORS: Black scuff marks should come right off if you rub them with a paper towel. If that doesn't work, sprinkle baking soda on a dampened sponge and scrub. Rinse with water.

SHOWER CURTAIN (PLASTIC): Toss into the washing machine with an old towel to provide scrubbing action. Add 1 cup white vinegar during rinse cycle. Hang to dry.

SHOWER DOORS (GLASS): To get rid of spots, wipe with a sponge dipped in white vinegar.

SHOWER DOORS (METAL FRAMES): To eliminate water spots on metal frames around shower doors or enclosures, lemon oil furniture polish or plain old mineral oil should do the job.

SHOWERHEAD: To remove mineral deposits, remove the head if possible and soak in warm vinegar, or fill a plastic sandwich bag with vinegar. Then wrap it around the showerhead and tie tightly with a rubber band. Allow it to sit overnight. Use an old toothbrush to scrub it clean. Poke with a pin or toothpick to clean the holes.

SHOWER WALLS AND FLOOR: Use a sponge mop that has been dunked into a bucket containing a solution of ½ cup vinegar, 1 cup clear ammonia and ¼ cup baking soda in 1 gallon of water. Rub around entire surface then rinse with clear water. CAUTION: Do NOT try to remove stains on porcelain tile or fiberglass with abrasive powders or steel-wool pads, because they'll scratch.

SILVER: Of course, you can use a commercial cleaning product and follow directions or use the following home-style method. CAUTION: DO NOT use this method on antique, silver plate or hollow handled pieces because it may cause damage. Also, only use this old-fashioned method *occasionally* and be aware that it may remove the "patina" (soft luster caused by tiny scratches that come with frequent use) from intricate patterns.

1. Cover the bottom of a deep plastic or glass pan with a layer of aluminum foil.

2. Pour in 2 quarts of boiling water.

All Around the House

3. Add 2 teaspoons of baking soda and stir well till dissolved.

4. Place silver pieces into solution until tarnish disappears.

5. Rinse in warm water and polish dry.

SLATE FIREPLACE: To remove crayon marks, use an art-gum eraser. First, knead it to make more pliable. Press against the marks to pull them off. Knead and press until all are gone.

STAINLESS STEEL: To remove rust that may be caused by mineral deposits or acidic foods left in the sink; rub stains with a paste of 3 parts baking soda, 1 part water. Rinse well. If the stains need further work, try a nonabrasive cleanser. Apply with a plastic scouring pad (do not use metal). Rub with the grain lines in the metal. Rinse well.

STAINLESS STEEL SINKS/COUNTERS: Clean with full-strength vinegar or a small amount of ammonia on a sponge, or baking soda on a damp sponge. Then put cooking oil on a paper towel and wipe further. Wipe dry to prevent water spots.

TEACUPS: To remove tea stains, mix a paste of baking soda and water. Rub it on the stains. Let stand for several minutes and wash as usual.

TEAKETTLE: (CAUTION: DO NOT use this method for electric kettles.) To eliminate lime buildup, fill kettle with full-strength vinegar and boil for several minutes, add some marbles to "bounce" and break up the sediment. Allow to stand then scrub if needed. Rinse well.

TELEPHONES: Wipe with an all-purpose spray on a paper towel or use wet towelettes to get rid of makeup or dirt. DO NOT spray the phone directly.

TELEVISION: Clean screen and cabinet with a soft, clean cloth. CAUTION: Do not use liquid or aerosol cleaners on the screen. As with all appliances, unplug before cleaning.

TOILET BOWL I: To remove lime buildup, first read the labels of liquid lime or hard water removers carefully because some warn against use on colored porcelain fixtures and are recommended only for white. Some lime and mineral removers can be used on both.

TOILET BOWL II: Here's a home-style hint. Pour full-strength vinegar into the bowl. Let stand for 5 minutes; scrub and flush. Never use harsh abrasives, steel wool, and steel scouring pads or pumice stones on porcelain or ceramic.

If the stains are really bad, try this: Remove the water from the bowl (turn off water valve to the tank and then flush until bowl is empty). Place white toilet paper over the badly discolored areas and saturate each with white vinegar. Let soak for a while. You may have to do this several times. Then scrub with a *plastic* brush to remove any remaining stain.

TOILET SEATS/LIDS: Clean plastic with a nonabrasive all-purpose cleaner. Rinse well. Dry hinge areas completely.

TUBS AND WASH BASINS: To remove rust stains from *porcelain*, rub with several cut lemons. If stain remains, make a paste of hydrogen peroxide and cream of tartar. Using an old toothbrush, scrub until stain is gone. Rust removers will do the job too, but rinse quickly with clean water, particularly on fiberglass tubs and basins.

For *fiberglass*, a paste of baking soda, water and cheap hair shampoo will clean well. CAUTION: Do not use abrasive cleaners because they scratch the finish. Once fiberglass is scratched, dirt becomes harder to remove and the scratch will remain visible. Wax fiberglass walls of a tub or shower stall (not the bottom!) with silicone car wax to restore the finish.

VARNISHED PANELING/WOODWORK: To get rid of fingerprints apply a solution of 1 part vinegar to 2 parts water with a clean cloth and wipe away. Polish with a clean, dry cloth.

VCRs: Use a commercial cleaner and follow directions precisely. Do not scrub, especially mechanical parts, because they can be damaged easily.

VINYL FLOOR: For light stains, vacuum or sweep up; then damp mop with warm water. Go over small areas at a time and rinse mop often so you don't smear dirt around. For really dirty floors, use a no-rinse cleaner or all-purpose liquid detergent. CAUTION: Do not use soap, gritty powders, or abrasive cleansers.

Darkened or yellowed areas caused by rubber- or vinyl-backed throw rugs placed on top of vinyl floors cannot be removed. That's because there is a chemical reaction between the backing of the throw rug and the vinyl flooring. Scrubbing and bleaching may lighten the stain a bit, but cannot remove it completely. Do not use abrasives because you may damage the finish on the vinyl. Placing other objects on top of this flooring can also cause yellowing. Do not leave any object in one spot on the floor for an extended time. Unfortunately, these stains cannot be removed.

VINYL FURNITURE: Clean with a mixture of mild detergent and water. Rub well to loosen dirt. Rinse and dry with a towel. If this is not successful, use commercial vinyl cleaners for difficult or greasy stains.

To remove *ballpoint ink stains*, dip a cotton swab into a bit of rubbing alcohol and carefully dab at the stain. Then wipe with a damp sponge.

VINYL SEAT CUSHION: Make a baking soda and water solution by mixing 4 tablespoons of baking soda and 1 quart warm water. Use a damp cloth or sponge to apply the solution, rinse and wipe dry.

> ### An Ounce of Prevention
> Automobile wax can be used to wax vinyl fabrics, which will help repel stains.

WAFFLE IRON: The grids can accumulate burned-on grease. To get rid of it, place an ammonia-soaked paper towel between top and bottom metal grids and leave overnight. If the grids are non-stick, follow manufacturer's instructions. Wash and rinse well.

WALLPAPER: Most wallpaper is now made of vinyl or vinyl-coated paper or cloth. Some marks can be removed with an art gum eraser or a wadded-up piece of fresh white bread. Test washability on a small inconspicuous spot first.

For *greasy marks*: If they won't come off with a cloth dampened with a diluted detergent solution, try a paste of baking soda and water. Apply it to the grease stain. Let dry and brush off with a soft cloth or brush.

For *ballpoint ink stains*, remove with rubbing alcohol (test on a hidden area first) by dabbing the alcohol on the stain with a cotton swab. You may have to repeat several times.

For *crayons*, eliminate by applying a prewash spray or dry-cleaning solvent with a cloth or sponge. Test first in a hidden area to make sure it doesn't stain. It may have to be repeated several times. A paste of baking soda mixed with water is a good cleaner too.

WALLS/DOORS: To remove sticky tape from painted surfaces, apply petroleum-based prewash spray or mineral oil to the tape. Leave for several minutes and remove. Start at a corner and work the tape loose. If needed, use more spray or oil, particularly if there are layers.

WALLS I: To patch *nail holes in colored walls*, fill with moistened crushed aspirin or white toothpaste and then dab area with watercolor paint to match the color. If you have leftover paint, use it.

WALLS II: To mask the discoloration caused by *nail holes in white walls*, fill with moistened crushed aspirin or white toothpaste; push into holes. Wipe off any excess with clean, damp cloth.

WALLS III: Simply painting over *water and oil stains* will not cover them, even if many coats of paint are applied. The stains will bleed through. First, the stains have to be painted over with a sealer product sold in paint stores. Clear varnish will work, too.

For *small ink stains*, "white" them out with correction fluid to seal then paint over.

For *water stains* in the ceiling, bleach them with 3 to 5 percent hydrogen peroxide, taking care to avoid any drips. Sometimes it's possible to mask spots with white shoe polish or correction fluid. If it doesn't work, use commercial stain sealer and repaint. (See also CEILING.)

WALLS IV: A bit of foam bathroom cleaner or dry-cleaning solvent will remove crayon marks from semi-gloss or glossy paint. Follow directions on cleaner container labels.

WINDOW BLINDS (bamboo): Dust and clean only with a soft hand brush or brush attachment of vacuum cleaner. Do not wash with water, or use citric based cleaners.

WINDOW BLINDS (wood): Put old clean socks on your hands and wipe on both sides of slats to clean dust or remove dust with the brush attachment of vacuum cleaner. Apply furniture polish to the slats or a creamy liquid wax.

WINDOWS: For a quick cleanup, spritz windows with full-strength white household vinegar and wipe with crumpled newspaper or paper towel. Or, make a solution of equal parts of water, isopropyl rubbing alcohol and non-sudsing ammonia and to cut grease. Mix and put in a spray bottle and be sure to label it clearly. Dry them on the outside from right to left and on the inside, dry them up and down. That way you will be able to determine whether any remaining streaks are inside or out. To make windows sparkle, add ½ to 1 cup vinegar to ½ gallon water. Put solution into a spray bottle and apply to windows. Dry well.

WINDOWS (salty accumulation): If you live near the ocean, the breezes bring salt that sticks to your windows. Spray full-strength white vinegar on the windows (not on the window frames). Allow it to stand for several minutes and then scrub with sponge covered with nylon net. Dry with paper towels or crumpled newspaper. Yes, you may end up with ink on your hands if you don't wear rubber gloves, but the windows will sparkle!

WINDOWS/STORM DOORS (plastic/vinyl): Use only a cleaning product formulated for plastics and vinyls. Some household cleaners and/or ammonia could cause a streaking in the plastic.

WOOD KITCHEN CABINETS: To remove grease—assuming that the woodwork is finished and also washable—use a wood cleaner and follow cleaning directions carefully. Then polish or wax with a soft cloth.

If the cabinets are *unfinished wood*, any kind of a cleaning substance including water could damage the surface, so rub grease off with a soft, dry cloth.

If the cabinets are *wood laminate*, lightly spray with a non-abrasive non-citric all-purpose cleaner. Let it stay on for several seconds, then sponge off.

WOOD PATIO FURNITURE: To remove mildew caused from setting out in weather (non-flood conditions) you will need to use a chlorine bleach and water solution. (Note: First, test the solution on a hidden area to make sure it does not discolor the furniture.) Make the solution by mixing ¾ cup of chlorine bleach and 1 gallon of water. Apply to the furniture and keep wet for 5 to 10 minutes. Rinse well and let air-dry completely.

WOOD SALAD BOWL: Hand wash the bowl with a solution of warm water and a mild liquid dishwashing detergent. Rinse and dry well. To help restore its original finish, wipe the entire surface with a layer of mineral oil and let set overnight. Wipe with paper towels to remove any excess oil.

WOOD SURFACES: To cover *shallow scratches* or small rings use the meat of several pecans or walnuts. Break meat in half and rub it on the scratches with your finger until it feels warm. The scratches should disappear in about 30 seconds. Wood stain that matches the coloring of the paneling can be rubbed into the scratch and then wiped with a clean cloth. Test on a hidden area first.

For *deep scratches or cracks* in wood, use wax sticks made for that purpose. Available at hardware stores, they come in a variety of colors to match most wood finishes. Rub into a crack until the wax is flush with the surface. Heat a putty knife in hot water and then use the flat side to press it across the area to get a smooth surface.

To remove *white rings* on most wood furniture (from hot mugs or wet glasses) try one of the following (CAUTION: DO NOT use on unfinished, lacquered or antique furniture.):

All Around the House

- Apply a mixture of mayonnaise with tobacco ash (cigar is the best) with a clean dry cloth.

- Use a non-gel toothpaste and baking soda mix. Rub gently until warm; it may take time for marks to disappear.

- Rub furniture wax into the wood with very fine steel wool.

Wax the wood when you have finished.

WOOD TRIM: Clean with a dusting product that can be sprayed on the cloth or directly on the surface. The newer "antistatic" or "electrostatic" microfiber cloths work well. Add shine by applying furniture cleaner or polish to surface. Wipe with a clean, soft cloth.

VARNISHED WOODWORK/PANELING: To remove fingerprints, wipe stained area with a solution of 1 part vinegar to 2 parts water, then polish with a dry cloth to restore luster.

Index

Index

Index